Syman

Children of Regar III

Alex Rae

Editor: Brenda Wright

Cover design © 2019 by P. W. Bledsoe and Sherrie Sanchez

Boat Tiger Books

Paperback ISBN: 978-0-9984633-5-3
Ebook ISBN: 978-0-9984633-4-6

Table of Contents

Cast

Jaika's Home on Regar – The City of Palon
The Ground Dwellers

Merith—Jaika's father and king of the city of Palon. His wife was killed by Kaleus and his marauders. To protect his daughter, he used Galimar and the SolStone to send Jaika to Earth.

Keshar—Captain of the Guard and father to Richard. He is a fearless fighter and would give his life for Merith and the people of Palon.

Galimar—One of Merith's Guardians of the Temple. Originally a soldier, he bears the scars of battle and the death of Merith's Queen. Forever Jaika's protector.

Richard—Keshar's son and best friend to Jaika. He has loved Jaika since they were children playing beneath the Manchura trees.

Inita—Caregiver who gave her life to see Jaika safely to Earth.

Kaleus—Now King of Devant. Once controlled by Oberon, he seeks to destroy Merith and Palon and all who serve there.

Oberon—The leader of the Guardians of the Temple. He fights to destroy all that Merith loves. He believes the SolStone holds the answers and seeks to control it and anyone else who can help him.

Ilea's Home on Regar – The City of Luz
The Tal

Sela—Mother to Ilea and Dodgen. A seer of patterns, she understands all languages ever spoken. She works for Oberon to try and rescue Ilea.

Adolphus—Father to Ilea and Dodgen. Courageous and strong, he fights against the cruelty in Palon. He is part of the Tal council and believed to be dead.

Dodgen—Ilea's brother. Although he struggles with a misshapen wing, Dodgen is courageous and a protector of the weak, just like his father Adolphus.

Kayz—Best friend to Dodgen. He is scattered, fearful, and unpredictable but forever loyal.

Ramon—A member of the Tal Council led by Sofos. Ramon has defied the council to search for Adolphus.

Tori—A healer who can see Lifesongs much like Ilea. Together with Tori, Argia, and Zaharra, each morning they sing their songs of healing to the city of Luz.

People of Earth

Nick—Jaika's dearest friend on Earth. He is brilliant and tenacious and will never stop until he finds her.

Jack—Nick and Jaika's friend on Earth. Strong and tough, he sees the good in all things and is forever hungry.

Rosie—Friends to Nick and Jack and Jaika. Because Rosie serves in the military, she is their inside source for otherwise secret information.

Mattie—A retired teacher who became Jaika's mother while she was on Earth. They were together until Jaika returned to Regar.

Prologue

Regar is a world once guided by a prophet. A prophet who foretold of a dark-eyed princess who could destroy kings and bring peace to Regar.

The moons of Regar
Shall future see
A dark-eyed princess
Come to thee

Born of power
Raised of ruin
Fed by prophets
Her nature turned

Her heart to Regar
Peace will bring
But serve destruction
To the lesser king

Syman

A dark-eyed daughter, Jaika, was born to King Merith of Palon. Men so believed in the prophecy that Merith was forced to hide his young daughter. Using the SolStone, Galimar sent her to Earth, where among friends, she learned and loved and grew to be a woman. Mattie, Jack, Nick, and Rosie were her entire world until Oberon brought her back to Regar with the power of the SolStone. He had taken control of Kaleus and now brought the dark-eyed princess home. With those she loved best left behind on Earth, Jaika would harden her heart and learn to fight and escape and eventually battle alongside her father against Oberon at the crystal mine … against Kaleus.

But Regar is a world of many stories, many lives. While Jaika lived on Earth, Ilea, a blue-skinned Tal, was captured by Kaleus's soldiers. She and her brother Dodgen were imprisoned at Devant, leaving their father's half-dead body at the crystal mine … leaving Adolphus in the crumbling rocks by the sheer cliffs of the mine. While she and her brother sat in prison, Kayz and his friends searched for Adolphus.

When Ilea and Dodgen tried to escape, Oberon again used the SolStone and sent Ilea to Earth. But Ilea was no ordinary Tal. She used her gifts to heal and destroy and to open a doorway back to Regar. She returned home bringing Jaika's friends, Jack and Nick, with her.

But before Jaika or Oberon, before Ilea or Dodgen or Kaleus, there was Syman. His story began long ago, and although neither Jaika nor Ilea have ever met Syman, he will bring them together. He will show them a secret world with creatures unlike any others. The iridescent Luna and the half-man, half-saktar Zaldi. But before Syman's story can be told, before he can bring them together, Adolphus must be found. Before Jaika can battle at the crystal mines, before Oberon can be carried out into the endless sand by the Breen, and before Ilea can be sent to Earth, the search for Adolphus must be completed. The story of Syman begins as Jaika's time on Earth is ending and Ilea's fight to escape the prison at Devant is beginning. Ilea sits in prison while those she left behind search for her father, Adolphus. At the edge of the cliffs by the crystal mine, they fly over the rocks to search for his body.

Finding Adolphus

Beneath the red moon of Regar, four blue-skinned Tal flew across the open sand. Tori and Ramon flew crisscross patterns across the ground. Kayz paused to wave Seela onward as she broke away from the group. She would continue alone to the city of Devant with hopes of rescuing her children, Ilea and Dodgen. They had been taken prisoner by the soldiers at the mine. The crystal mine that Seela had known nothing about. But Kayz would continue with the others. He and Tori and Ramon would fly back to the crystal mine to find Seela's husband ... to find Adolphus ... or at least what was left of him.

Seela did not look behind her as she left the group. She tried her best not to imagine what they might find. Her lifesong ached for her husband. She asked the creator Gelquin to protect him ... to protect them all. In her heart she knew he would forgive her for not stopping to say goodbye. The red moon would be her only companion on the journey to Devant.

Syman

The morning winds stirred the sand as the first rays of sunlight glowed along the horizon. Kayz, Tori, and Ramon had finally reached the crumbling rocks that marked the border of the sand and the mountains and the steep cliffs that overlooked the crystal mine. They searched from the sky, looking for signs of Adolphus. He had been down there a very long time. Their hope that he was still alive grew smaller with each beat of their wings. Frustrated, they landed in the open sand then made their way to the fallen rocks at the edge of the cliffs to begin searching on foot.

"I know this is the place I left him," Kayz growled as he climbed across the rocks, his blue wings twitching. He was the youngest in the group, but he was the only one who had been here when Adolphus fell. It was up to him to lead the way. He dug in the sand where Adolphus should have been. He could still see the indentions where the body had rested and the clumps of sand where his blood had dried in patches.

"The crystals," he almost yelled, scooping them up from the sand. "Here are the crystals I gave him to hold!"

Tori stared at the blood, cracked and dried on the side of the crystals, then reached out to take one from Kayz. "What did you do with this crystal?" She ran her fingers along the edges, watching its light shimmer between her fingers and feeling the hum within. *I wish Ilea was here. She is so much stronger ... she could find her father. What if I cannot heal him? What if ...*

Kayz looked away, remembering that night at the mine ... remembering the fear and the tightness in his chest. Adolphus had been shot and Ilea and Dodgen taken while he sat frozen, terrified, powerless to help them. He had been a coward. "I dragged him behind the rocks then I put the crystals in his hands ... in Adolphus's hands. I told him to think of his daughter, Ilea ... and the crystals glowed ... just a little ... but his breathing became stronger. I know he was getting stronger. I had to leave him. I couldn't lift him. It was the only way. Maybe he tried to go home. Do you think he was strong enough? He could still be alive ... somewhere."

Tori listened to Kayz chatter and felt for lifesongs in the sand and the rocks and the crystals, wishing again that Ilea was by her side. "Someone else has been here. That is all I can feel."

Kayz's shoulders dropped in defeat. "No!" He screamed to the dawn. "Adolphus! Where are you?" He flailed his wings. "Talk to the crystals, Tori. Find Adolphus. I know you can find him."

"It doesn't work like that," said Tori. "I wish it did." Her eyes searched the blood-stained sand. "Let's go up. Maybe I can see him."

6

"This is my fault," Kayz moaned.

"No," Tori touched his shoulder. "There is darkness in the ground dwellers that you cannot stop. Darkness that rails against the light." She sighed in exhaustion. "Our light holds it back, but the darkness returns."

Kayz nodded and stiffened his shoulders. "Darkness ... alright, let's go up."

"Yes, up ... I want to go up." Ramon spoke for the first time since they had landed. While the others had chatted, he had been searching the rocks beyond ... the places where someone could hide. His years of experience had taught him patience and the futility of working without a plan.

Tori and Kayz turned and stared. They had forgotten about Ramon. Kayz chuckled to himself. *Tall, dark-haired, handsome Ramon ... older and wiser but I am still faster.*

"Ramon, what do you see?" Tori felt strange working side by side with a council member. They had seldom spoken before they began searching for Adolphus, so discussing what to do felt awkward and out of place.

"It's not so much what I see as what I feel." His voice was soft but firm. "There is power up there."

Tori nodded. She had felt the power wavering in the cliffs, but it was not Adolphus. Ramon did not have the gift of healing or seeing life the way she did ... the way Ilea could ... but he often saw what others missed.

Kayz didn't understand, but anything was better than just sitting here agonizing over what might have happened.

Ramon began climbing. Hand and foot and claw, he climbed over the rocks and made his way toward the sheer cliffs beyond. His wings lifted him above the stones in places no ground dweller could pass. With each step, with each wing shift, he kept watch among the stones for Adolphus. Kayz and Tori stayed close behind.

"There!" Tori yelled. "I see blood."

Kayz rolled his eyes. They had not seen Adolphus and his injuries. He could never have made it this far ... at least not alone.

Tori hooked her claws into the side of a stone the height of two men and hung from the edge. She ran her fingers over the blood and the sticky white substance beside it. "He is not alone. There is someone else with him." She didn't know how to explain to them that the *someone else* felt more like a living crystal than a person. The tips of her fingers that had touched the sticky goo tingled with life. "So much light," she whispered to the stones.

"So, let's keep going," Kayz urged, feeling a little annoyed at the delay.

"Yes," Ramon agreed. "Let's keep going."

Tori rose above the stone and into the sky still holding one of the blood-caked crystals. The pale light of the morning sun was beginning to streak the jagged rocks and the side of the cliffs, and the trail of Adolphus glowed beneath it. The tiniest drops of blood blended with the sticky goo and made a trail of light into the highest parts of the mountain. "There," she pointed to the upper levels. "We have to go there."

Kayz threw his head back and launched his body into the air. It felt good to fly, but he couldn't shake the sickening feeling that this sticky goo might be saliva from a hungry animal. Maybe Adolphus had not come this way at all, but only his half-chewed carcass dragged by a monster. A creature that could easily climb these jagged rocks.

Tori flew behind him, diving into the rocks and then rising again, moving higher and deeper into the mountain range.

Kayz fought his impatience and rose higher into the sky. His teeth clenched, his shoulders twitched, and his wings carried him high above Tori and Ramon, high above the mountains. He growled low and cursed himself for being ordinary. Tori and Ilea and even the fearless Ramon had skills that could save lives … that could make a difference. He, however, was just Kayz, just a plain, ordinary Tal. And on top of that, he was a coward.

He spiraled and swirled and then he saw it. Beyond the highest peak, the mountain curved and dipped and leveled. Where there should be no light, Kayz could see a soft glow. He spun and flew back toward Tori. "There's a light," he shouted, gasping and sputtering.

He flew in circles around her, above and below. "A light … I see a light!"

Tori kept studying the cliffs, ignoring Kayz and his chatter. So, he flew closer. Their wings scraped together, and Tori cried out in pain as she dropped the crystal.

"Listen to me!" Kayz shouted.

"Be careful!" Tori shouted back, hovering and glaring at Kayz.

"Somebody is up there!" Kayz waved for her and Ramon to follow, then led them toward the highest peak.

10

Syman

The three of them spiraled and flew to the landing beside the glow and an entrance to a cave. Tori could feel the twisting and turning of the passageways inside the mountain and the power that waited within. She closed her eyes and quieted her breathing to find the source of the power, the source of the glow. She reached out her lifesong to meet with whatever ... whoever ... lived inside the cave. Somewhere inside, she hoped to find Adolphus.

Kayz and Ramon watched as her hands shook. Her fingers twitched in pulsating rhythm. "Krill," she whispered, "Krill."

Her wings spread wide as she threw back her head and screamed. Her eyes closed, and her body crumpled. Ramon threw his arms around her waist to break her fall. She hung limp in his grasp ... her blue wings trailing the ground.

"She will be alright," a voice announced from the cave.

Ramon lifted Tori from the ground and turned with Kayz to see Adolphus standing in the entrance. His skin a deep blue and his wings folded around his body in proper Tal fashion. He was healthy and strong, but his eyes were lifeless and gray.

"Why have you come?"

11

"We were looking for you!" Kayz shouted, scampering up the cliff to look down over the others. "We came to find you."

"I was dead," Adolphus explained, looking up at Kayz. "Thank you for trying to help me." His words were flat and without feeling.

Tori squirmed in Ramon's grasp, and he laid her onto the rocky floor. "That isn't Adolphus," she whimpered as she sat up and tried to shake the shadows from her mind. "You're not Adolphus."

"I *am* Adolphus," he said. "I will show you." He turned, sending the tails of his wings swirling behind him, then walked back into the cave.

Ramon helped Tori to her feet. She leaned against him as they followed Adolphus. Kayz stayed close to the top of the cave walls, climbing and jumping over unwelcoming rocks, using his wings to carry him up and around the ceiling, refusing to return to the ground.

As they moved deeper into the cave, the craggy walls became covered with red, glowing vines that crawled and wound around the hanging spears of rock that jutted out from the ceiling and floor. The air was crisp and clean and shimmered with the light that came from the plants and the life deep within the cavern.

"Be careful where you step," Tori warned. "Don't step on the plants."

"Don't step on the plants," Ramon complained. "How am I supposed to move without stepping on the plants?"

"They feel pain," Tori warned again. "At least try."

Kayz clawed at a loose vine hanging from the ceiling to see if it would make any noise. While below him, Ramon and Tori walked deeper into the cave, toward the increasing light.

"We are Krill," Adolphus explained as he led them deeper into the mountain. "And there is much work to do."

Tori didn't know who this Krill was, but she frowned at the idea of him being in control of Adolphus. As they walked, she could feel the ground moving beneath her. Tentacles twitching and jerking and withdrawing deeper into the cave. This Krill was everywhere.

"We protect," Adolphus continued his explanation.

"Of course you do," Ramon said watching Kayz skitter across the cave walls and ceiling like some tree creature. "But who protects us from you?"

Tori paused and reached down to touch one of the tentacles that wiggled and twisted from her grasp. Her lifesong felt the wave of power and the weary purpose that weighed on the creature connected to the tentacle ... the Krill.

As they turned the final corner in the maze of tunnels, the tentacles pulled together to join beneath a mound of flesh with round leafy-green eyes. Eyes as large as a man's hand. Adolphus stood beside him.

"We are Krill," the creature spoke without a mouth. The massive body began to shrink as the tentacles coiled beneath it, creating the illusion of a head and torso. Its eyes narrowed, and a mouth formed beneath. "Is this more ... comfortable?"

"You are with Adolphus," Tori was beginning to understand.

"Yes," the Krill answered. "He was lost to you. I could not save his body, so we became one. He is Adolphus, and I am Adolphus."

Kayz dropped from the ceiling. "So, you are inside him?" He squirmed with the thought of those tentacles creeping inside his ears and throat.

Tori shook her head. "No, Kayz. He keeps him alive. Adolphus has part of the Krill's lifesong in him. They are together."

14

Syman

Adolphus turned and looked at Tori. She could feel the mix of life inside him. "You are still father to Dodgen and Ilea, are you not?"

"Yes … yes," his eyes swirled with flecks of blue. "Where are they?" his voice cracked with the words and Tori could feel his body growing weaker. "Where are my children?" The Krill released his hold on Adolphus, setting his lifesong free to speak. "Where are they?"

"I don't know." Kayz's shoulders slumped with the full burden of his cowardice. "I don't know. They were taken … at the mines … the night you were …" He started to say killed, but that wasn't true. "The soldiers took them to Devant. Seela went to find them."

"Seela," Adolphus closed his eyes for a moment. His strength and the Krill returned to his lifesong. "He will be here soon." Adolphus opened his eyes to stare at Kayz. "He will come to find me."

"He?" Ramon didn't like the idea of more strange creatures showing up.

"Dodgen," Adolphus's eyes sparkled for an instant. "He will be here soon, and then we will leave for Luz."

"How can you possibly know that?" Tori studied his lifesong for any signs that he was lying, but there was nothing.

"We are in Devant," Adolphus explained. "The Krill is in Devant. We have been here ... since the beginning."

Dodgen Returns

Tori, Ramon, and Kayz spent the rest of the day pacing and flying and waiting. If there was a chance that Dodgen was coming, they would wait as long as necessary.   Ramon didn't remember ever hearing stories about the Krill or beings that could share their lifesong. Even Sofos had never spoken of such a creature. He and Tori tried asking questions, but Adolphus had no answers. He sat in meditation beside the Krill. Not speaking or moving or doing anything helpful. But as the sun began to set, as promised, Dodgen arrived. Tori could feel the odd flight pattern created by his crippled wing as he approached the mine, so she flew out to meet him.

As she guided him to the ledge at the opening of the cave where the others waited, Dodgen began sharing his stories of Devant and Oberon. He told his friends of the prison where he had been held with his sister, Ilea, and how she had destroyed their chains and the locks on the cell doors so they could escape. He described Oberon and his use of the blue stone to send

Ilea to a place they couldn't go. And Seela … his mother … he told them of her bravery. How she stayed with Oberon so that he could go free. She agreed to remain if Oberon would find Ilea … if he would use the blue stone to bring Ilea home.

Kayz's eyes grew wide. "We should go and save your mother!"

Dodgen shook his head. "She agreed to stay. I need to give her a chance … she can make him bring Ilea back. I know she can."

Dodgen collapsed onto the ground. His heart aching. His body quivering from fear and exhaustion. Tori sat down beside him and put her hand on his. Softly, she began to sing, weaving her lifesong into his, giving him strength. He leaned against her, welcoming her gift of healing. Dodgen thought of Tori's daughter and how terrified she would be if she knew the truth about where they were and all that was happening. As he drank in her warmth, Dodgen made a silent vow. *I will not let your daughter lose you as I have lost my mother.*

Kayz flopped down beside them, sitting on his hands to keep them still. "I need to show you something." Kayz pushed back the guilt of leaving his friend behind, of not being able to save Adolphus. The pain of his cowardice gnawed at his stomach like a hungry Breen, but he forced himself to focus on what needed to happen next.

Dodgen smiled over at Kayz, his strength building with Tori's light.

Kayz held out his hand. "You really need to see this."

Tori shook her head no, but Kayz ignored her. The Tal boys locked hands and Dodgen stood on shaky legs. Kayz didn't have the words to explain, so he led him deep inside the cave to the tentacled Krill and Adolphus sitting in meditation.

"Father!" Dodgen crumpled to the ground. "I knew you were alive."

Kayz gripped his friend by the upper arm. "He's not the same. But he's still in there … somewhere. I wanted you to know he was still alive."

Adolphus opened his eyes. "My son, I am pleased to see you are well." He did not stand or uncross his hands that lay cupped in his lap. He stared at his son for a moment and then closed his eyes again.

"Father! Please!" Dodgen stood then crept closer to Adolphus. "What's wrong with you?" His arms and legs tingled with fear and excitement and exhaustion.

Tori appeared out of the darkness to put her hand on Dodgen's shoulder. "He was dying. The Krill … this thing with endless legs … it saved him." She did her best to numb his pain with her lifesong as she spoke. "But … it changed him." She squeezed his shoulder and quieted her voice. "Come away from this place," she whispered. "This thing is not your father."

Dodgen's anger softened as he once again connected with Tori's light. She began to sing as she led him away, glaring at Kayz as they passed. Her voice echoed throughout the stone cavern. Her fingers massaging, caressing, working to quiet Dodgen's fear. "Come and rest for a while. You will feel better after you rest."

Close to the opening of the cave, Tori settled on the stone ground along with Dodgen. Kayz followed to sit fidgeting across from them. He wanted to explain. He wanted to say he was sorry, but this wasn't the time. He knew that. Ramon joined them on the ground, oblivious to Dodgen and his pain.

There, at the entrance to the cave, they spent the night, half-sleeping, half-watching the shadows. Kayz kept dreaming of the perfect moment to speak with Dodgen about that night at the mine. The night he had hidden like a coward. The night the soldiers had taken Ilea. But there never seemed to be a right time nor the right words.

Syman

Adolphus sat frozen in meditation beside the tentacled Krill until the sun's rays lit the sky, then he rose and stretched and walked to the opening of the cave only to stop and watch the sun's light brighten the sky. His eyes still gray. The others lay on the ground behind him, somewhere between asleep and awake. "We must warn the people. They must prepare." He announced.

Tori and Dodgen stretched and tried to remember where they were. Ramon walked out onto the platform in front of the cave to stand with Adolphus. He wanted to believe this version of his friend. He wanted to believe that he was alive and ready to help, but this could be a trick. The Tal had enemies everywhere. He must not allow this creature to come back into his city without being sure.

"Who *are* the people and exactly what are they preparing for?" Ramon approached the situation as a councilman. "Can you explain?"

Tori stepped out into the light to listen. On instinct, her lifesong reached out to Adolphus to confirm her findings from the day before. Nothing had changed within him. The Krill controlled his body and yet Adolphus still lingered in the background.

Adolphus glanced over his shoulder to acknowledge her presence. "Your world is ending. You must prepare the people."

"The Tal?" Tori asked, rubbing the sleep from her eyes.

"Everyone must prepare."

Dodgen listened as they talked, not sure of what to say. He just stared at his father and tried to make sense of it all. *Why doesn't he seem to know me?*

Ramon shook his head. "What do you mean everyone? Prepare for what?"

Adolphus closed his eyes and took a deep breath. His chest bulged and tightened beneath his tunic. As he exhaled, the ground began to shake. Tori stumbled to the side of the cave then dug her claws into the rocks to keep from falling. Dust and crumbling stone burned her eyes. Ramon knelt and anchored himself to the ground with his claws. His wings wrapped around his shoulders and head like a shield. Dodgen gripped the floor and watched his father in disbelief.

"Everybody get out!" Kayz shrieked as he ran, stumbling out of the cave to dive into the open air. His wings carried him to a safe distance where he hovered and watched the others clinging to the mountain as it swayed.

When the shaking stopped, Adolphus turned to Ramon still gripping the ground. "All creatures will be destroyed once the Krill leave."

Ramon and Tori stood, their hearts pounding in their chests.

Adolphus looked at each of them, studying their reactions. "Now you understand."

"I don't understand." Dodgen shouted as he flexed his claws. He wanted to be happy that his father was alive, but he felt only anger at this thing ... this thing his father had become.

Adolphus turned toward his son, and for a heartbeat, the gray of his eyes showed blue. "Do not be afraid," he mumbled. Then the gray returned.

Ramon shook his head. He didn't understand any of this. *Adolphus seemed to have the power to destroy the mountains. Maybe Adolphus is being used. Maybe he is trying to warn us that the Krill is evil. Why would he want to destroy Regar?*

"I will help you make preparations." Adolphus didn't wait for Ramon to ask any of his questions. "I will leave the other body so that I can come with you." He waived his hand toward the opening of the cave.

Syman

Tori felt the tentacled body deep in the mountain collapse. Its lifesong quieted while the song of Adolphus grew stronger. He felt no pain or joy, just a shift in his lifesong. He took a deep breath and then opened his wings. They curled forward as he dove from the ledge. The *Vhoom* of his Tal wings shook the air as he rose into the sky. Kayz dropped, then spiraled skyward to follow. Ramon nodded to Tori, then his wings opened to follow as well.

Dodgen looked at Tori for answers, but she was afraid to speak. She wanted to shout, to tell him what happened, what she had felt, but she didn't think he would believe her. She wanted to explain that the other body … the body inside the cave was dead. That the light within it now flew with Adolphus. That he was carrying the full power and strength of that tentacled creature to their home. He was carrying the ability to destroy their mountain.

Instead she offered a quiet smile and her hand. "Let's go home," she pleaded. "They are going to need us."

Battle for the Crystal Mine

In Luz, they waited 124 suns. With each new sun Adolphus would meet with the elders and those on the council. He would speak with Ramon and Sofos and Zaharra and Argia. He told them of the coming dangers, but they did not believe. He shook the mountain again and again, still they did not believe. The council told stories of past tremors in the cliffs that had sent rocks falling into the city. They spoke of battles and failed attacks on the city of Luz. Whatever Adolphus believed was coming, their city would never be destroyed.

On the morning of the 124th sun, Adolphus tried again. To convince the Tal elders that he could see coming events, he foretold of a battle that would rage in the desert by night fall.

"At this moment, King Merith of Palon travels with his soldiers to the crystal mines to battle for the prisoners inside," he explained. "I cannot predict the outcome, but a part of me exists in Palon as well as

25

Devant, so I know this to be true. Come with me, and I will prove to you that I speak the truth."

Sofos dismissed him saying that the crystal mines were not their concern, but many of the others were beginning to doubt the wisdom of the old council members. So, beneath the yellow sun and the red moon, Adolphus led a handful of believers to the crystal mines. Dodgen, Tori, Ramon, and Kayz flew with them. They already knew the way.

The last rays of the sun filtered across the mountains as they landed in the cliffs above the crystal mines. Dodgen sat down with his legs hanging off a rocky ledge and his crooked wing tucked up against his back. He could see the guards outside the opening to the mine below. This was the place he and Ilea had been captured. This was the place Adolphus had been killed and changed. This was a place he never wanted to see again.

Kayz sat down on the cliff beside his friend, pushing his wings out behind him. "Forgive me," he whispered to Dodgen. "Please ... forgive me."

Dodgen squinted at his friend. "What have you done now?"

Kayz shook his head. "I left you here ... down there ... I let Kaleus's soldiers take you ... and Ilea."

Finally, he had said it. The words he had wanted to say for so long.

Dodgen jabbed his friend in the side with his elbow. "They would have killed you. If you had attacked, you'd be dead. There's nothing to forgive."

Kayz knew this would be the last they would speak of it. Dodgen had forgiven him but forgiving himself would take much longer. He closed his eyes and thanked Gelquin for his friend's safe return and wondered if they would ever find Ilea. If he would ever have a chance to ask for her forgiveness as well. He sat there beside his friend waiting and whispering and watching the yellow moon shifting in the sky for what seemed like forever. Then the shadows between the rocks began to move.

"Look!" ordered Adolphus. "Along the rocks ... Merith's soldiers."

The Tal waited along the cliffs watching the men below. In the light of the torches and the glowers that lined the opening to the mine, Tori watched as a pair of soldiers killed one guard and then the other. She could almost feel the metal in the sword as it was driven into his heart.

Two by two the soldiers crept from the rocks and the shadows to enter the crystal mines. Ramon listened to the quiet *ffft* of their burn guns that flickered within the cave. Still more soldiers came from the far side of the mine. Soldiers dressed in black. Just as the others, these men made no sound.

"Should we help them?" Tori asked. She wanted to scream. To tell the soldiers to let the prisoners go. That the Tal would defeat them.

"No," Adolphus warned. "There are others who will help."

The mine was quiet for a while. The Tal grew restless, shifting their positions, standing, sitting, climbing higher and lower on the cliffs. Some drifted off to sleep against the stone. But Dodgen never moved. He gripped the rock and hung ready to launch in a heartbeat. He couldn't shake the thought that Ilea might be in there. As the night passed, men and women and children of all species staggered from the bowels of the mine. First only a few, but their numbers grew. Empty, hollow people who could barely stand. Soldiers in gray walked with them. Some embracing. Some even carrying the weaker prisoners.

Tori sat down beside Kayz and Dodgen. "I don't understand." Her heart ached with the sadness and frailty of the people below. "I want to help them. There are in so much pain."

Kayz wrapped his arm around her shoulder. "Ilea wanted to help them too. But what can we do for them?" He could hear himself mocking Ilea on the night they had come here to steal the crystals. *Where will they go? The prisoners will just wonder around in the sand.* He should have been fearless. He should have protected everyone.

Tori tried to shut out their pain. "When the soldiers are gone ... maybe then."

"Maybe then," Kayz agreed.

The sun's rays glistened across the sand as Ramon stood and stretched. "What is happening now?" He rubbed his neck, weary from lack of sleep.

"Listen!" Kayz growled. "I hear them."

Soldiers ran from the rocks. Soldiers in black rushed to surround the entrance to the cave. Ten or twelve made their way inside, but the rest stood watch outside the mine.

Ramon heard that same *ffft* of gun fire. Then shouting ... men screaming out in pain. The sounds of war erupted from the mines out onto the sand. A man in black dragged a young soldier by the hair out into the light. He pressed a gun to the soldier's neck shouting at the others.

"That soldier," Tori gasped. "That soldier is a girl."

Syman

Dodgen stood. "We have to help her!"

"Be patient," Adolphus assured him. "Help is coming."

They watched the scene below. The man in black shouted about a prophecy and a king. Two ground dwellers moved to face him in front of the crowd. One towering over the other. Then the prisoners began to make their way back into the mine. The soldiers in black forced them to return. Tori stood and growled as she felt them dying from gun fire.

"What is happening?" Ramon was standing behind them now.

"That man in black ... he was at the palace at Devant." Dodgen's wings flexed and he hung his claws over the ledge. "He is the man who took my mother ... Oberon."

He lifted his wings and prepared to fly, but Adolphus waved him back. "Look." He pointed to the sky. "Help is coming."

The Tal watched from the cliffs as a black wave of wings covered the sun. More Breen than they could count descended on the soldiers and the man in black. Dodgen and Kayz moved along the cliffs to get a better view. The Breen attack was quick. A fury of wings left many of the soldiers lifeless on the ground. The man in black was carried away by the powerful claws of the Breen.

Adolphus flew from the cliffs to lead the others back to Luz, but Dodgen and Kayz stayed behind. They sat high on the cliffs and watched until the last of the prisoners were taken from the mine. They watched with fading hope for Ilea.

Arrival

"She opened a portal!" Jack yelled. "It's a door … it's Jaika's door!"

Jack didn't wait for an answer. He wrapped his arms around his two friends and carried them toward the light.

Nick cried out, "What if Jaika's not there?"

Jack nodded and held his friends even tighter. "Then we will just have to open another door!" He walked forward through the doorway of light, carrying his friends with him.

Ilea gasped as Jack dropped her and Nick face-down into the sand. Spitting and sputtering she sat up and tried to catch her breath. The doorway behind them had vanished. Her head spun and her sight blurred. *The cave … where did the cave go? Why are we no longer in the cave? And the sand … so much sand?* Ilea's hands trembled. Her wings dropped against the ground. Her legs heavy and lifeless. She forced her body to work, making each part do their job. Her wings scooped the air to help her legs lift her body to stand. The sand stretched out before her and behind her, but to her right, that side was blocked by fierce, jagged mountains with steep slopes that rose up out of the ground as if they had been shoved from below. To her left, low on the horizon, a sliver of red peered out across the sand. A sliver of a red moon ... her red moon. She knew every bend and crevice and mark ... every detail of her red moon. She knew the vibrations in the sand and the sky and song of the sun. She was home. She was not close to Luz or even Palon, but she was in the world of the red moon. The moon was in the wrong place and she was in the wrong place. But if she could travel far enough, fly far enough, she would find her city of Luz and the blue-skinned Tal people she loved.

"Did we make it?" Nick whimpered, unable to stand. Blood oozed from his arm leaving a dark trail against the white sand.

"I think we should run!" Jack yelled.

To her left, Ilea could see Nick laying on the sand with Jack sitting up beside him. She followed Jack's gaze to the distant horizon behind her and to a dark winged creature flying toward them. Above the sand, about eye level, a heavy black creature with sharp teeth and glowing eyes raced toward them.

Syman

"That's a dragon," Jack muttered, scooting backward on the sand. "That's a dragon. Jaika never said anything about dragons in her world."

Ilea had never seen such a creature, but Jack … Jack had a name for this terrifying beast, and he was certain it would destroy them.

She could hear the *vhoom* of its wings thrashing against the air. Rhythmic beating, pounding against the air, stronger than any full-grown Tal she had ever known. Ilea ran forward, forcing her wings to open and catch the air. She advanced to meet this creature, this dragon. Out in front of her friends, she hovered at the same level as the beast. Her arms spread wide while her body hug down long and straight. Her wings sweeping back and forth, powerful slow movements to keep her body in place. Almost as if she was treading water in the air.

And then she screamed! "Aaaaahhhhhhhh!" A shrill, ear wrenching scream that tore at the air around her. Jack covered his ears and leaned across Nick who was growing weaker by the moment. Over and over she screamed.

The dragon locked eyes with Ilea as he approached and then turned his head to the side as if a great wind had forced him backward. He too began to hover, matching Ilea's movements. Sweeping his wings back and forth to maintain his position, dropping his tail and lowering his body beneath him. His tail touching the sand.

Jack could see Ilea and the dragon facing each other in midair, silently studying the other's movements. He felt like he was in a fairy tale or one of those science fiction movies that Nick loved to watch. A blue-skinned girl with short, white hair and translucent wings facing a dragon. A dragon with metallic scales and leathery wings that reached out at least three times as far as Ilea's. When the dragon opened his mouth to growl, Jack could see his dagger shaped teeth.

Ilea shrieked again … and the dragon exploded.

Ilea felt his lifesong shatter into a million shining pieces. Each piece carrying its own lifesong. She had never felt anything like him. The pieces swirled and danced and dropped and, before she could take another breath, they merged into a ground dweller. Ilea's wings twitched and slowed to lower her to the sand to face this confusing man. The metallic scales of the dragon had become a dark cloak. The dragon's head was now a man's face. A long narrow face with high cheekbones and no hair. His skin seemed to lack any color at all. Ghostly white, even translucent at times. Ilea could feel the voices inside him. The millions of lifesongs singing in unison, together but apart.

"Ilea!" Jack yelled, no longer worried about the dragon. "He's going to die."

Ilea turned to see Nick still laying on his back. The sand around his wrist was soaked black-red with his blood. She rushed to his side forgetting all about the dragon-man. She wrapped both hands around his wrist and pushed her lifesong into the open wounds. She shouted to the voices in his body to join and heal and as she spoke, she remembered. The way their bracelets had glowed and burned and opened the doorway to this place. How she had not be able to control the light and that she had caused these wounds.

The burns along his arm began to peel and flake away. She strengthened his lifesong to speed the healing and, when she removed her blood-soaked hands, the wound was sealed. She brushed her fingertips along his arm to rub away the blood.

"He cannot stay in the sun!" The dragon-man spoke in the Tal language. "We must move him inside."

They watched as the dragon-man moved closer then reached down toward Nick. Jack shoved his arm away. "You're not touching him!" he growled.

Syman

The dragon-man backed away as Jack picked up Nick's limp body. Holding his friend, he looked to Ilea for answers. "Where are we going?" he asked.

Ilea picked up Nick's glasses from the bloody sand, then once more, she let her lifesong search for darkness and danger inside the dragon who was now a man.

The dragon-man motioned for them to follow. Jack waited for Ilea to object, to say that they would find their own way, but she followed this creature toward the mountains. So he followed too.

There seemed to be no entrance or pathway into the infinite jagged cliffs that lined the edge of the sand. Only the sand, which ended abruptly at the base and bothered Jack for some odd reason. Nick would have had some explanation or theory, but Jack just didn't like it.

They followed the dragon-man along the cliffs for what seemed like forever. Trudging through the sand, each step taking more effort than the one before. The sun was getting hotter, and Nick was getting heavier. Jack's biceps burned from the weight of his friend's body. Then the dragon-man turned and disappeared. Ilea and Jack followed him through an opening in the cliff. A perfect arched doorway that had been cut from the stone. The doorway became a tunnel, at least twenty feet long climbing upward into the mountain with the same smooth cut ceiling and walls. The tunnel was lit by iridescent metallic columns on each side of the ramped floor. Each column cast a different color and was covered in laser perfect etchings of indescribable creatures. Jack studied the thin ruts cut into the edges of the flooring and wondered if they were for drainage, like on a bridge. Then he wondered what kind of tool could do such a thing and if the dragon-man had one and just how dangerous this guy might be. *Wake up Nick. I need your brain.*

Nick moaned, and Jack assured him everything was under control.

When Jack felt like his arms were ready to fall off, the tunnel opened out onto a plateau the size of a football field. Ilea was happy to be in the mountains once again. This place was closer to home than she had been in a long time. Jack kept hoping this place had a snack bar.

Doorways to rooms and caves were cut into the rock around the landing. People came out of their homes to stare at the newcomers. People put together in ways that Jack and Ilea had never seen before. People with green skin and yellow skin. Giants with white eyes and people no taller than a man's knee. Men and women with extra arms and legs and what looked like animal parts. Some creatures even glowed. A young girl had skin the same red color as the leaves of a Manchura tree. One creature, whose upper body was that of a man, a ground dweller, had a lower body of four legs and long shaggy fur like that of a saktar. Another man had four arms. Two were crossed in front of him in indignation, while one held the hand of a child who had only two arms.

In the middle of the landing stood a round, open-sided room with its stair-stepped metal roof supported by the same iridescent columns that had lined the tunnel. At the far end of the landing, Jack could see another ramp and thin ruts cut into its edges. Thin ruts that laced the plateau in uniform lines along the outer edges. *Drainage,* Jack thought. *This is a desert. Why do they need drainage? Does it ever rain here? Where is here? And why do I care. Wake up, Nick.*

The dragon-man led them to the first cave on the left side. "This is my home," he said to Ilea in the Tal language.

"I don't trust him," Jack mumbled.

The dragon-man straightened his shoulders and turned to look at Jack. "I will not harm you," he said in perfect English. "This is my home."

Syman

Ilea's eyes grew wide. *How could this man know Jack's language?* Her heart filled with doubt. *Maybe we are not on Regar after all.*

Inside the dragon-man's house, Ilea felt strangely at ease. This place reminded her of home. Floor mats woven from plant fibers covered the floors beneath backless benches here and there. A table and a firepit with a vent were next to the opening of the cave. A place for cooking and eating and sleeping and all the tools you need in a mountain home. The things Ilea would have in her home … but the dragon-man had so much more.

Jack laid Nick down on a wide bench, his body sinking into the cushion. A pillow covered with intricate patterns. Bright colors and designs woven from fibers and fluff to make a thick, welcoming mattress. The bench itself was decorated with deep scrollwork along the legs and arms and painted a brilliant green.

Above it hung a tapestry with the sky and the clouds and the mountains woven from the same fibers as the bench cushion. Ilea tried to image the time and tools it would have taken to create such a piece.

The dragon-man caught her staring at the bench and the wall hanging. "We have many artisans in our city," he said in the Tal language, and then repeated the words in English.

She stepped back toward the door. "How can you …?"

"I speak all known languages," the dragon-man stated.

Jack sat down on the bench beside Nick. "I'll just bet you do."

"Like my mother." Ilea tried to understand. "My mother can see the patterns in words and music."

"Perhaps," he said, then looked past her as if trying to decide what to say next. "I have not followed protocol." He bowed slightly, continuing to speak in English. "My name is Syman, and I welcome you to the Lost City."

"Lost is what we are," Jack agreed.

"The original name was City of the Lost, but over time the name was shortened to the Lost City." Syman looked at Jack. "It was built by the Maker."

"I'm Jack, this is Nick, and she's Ilea. Do you have anything to eat?" Jack's stomach rumbled.

"I am worried about my friend." Ilea had healed Nick's arm, but he was still weak from blood loss.

Syman

Syman looked at Nick. "He will be fine. You have already healed his wound."

Ilea didn't think this strange man understood. Maybe this Maker he spoke of could help. "Who is the Maker?" Ilea squinted. "Did the Maker make me? Can he help my friend?"

"No," Syman stated. "You were made by a male and female Tal."

Ilea rolled her eyes. *He is so frustrating.* "So, the Maker is Gelquin?"

Syman tilted his head slightly. His face was just as blank and unemotional as it had been since they arrived. "The Maker is the Maker."

Ilea's wings twitched with impatience.

Ilea still did not understand. He sounded as crazy as the council when they argued about past events, places and people, and battles that they all seem to remember differently.

"So, did the Maker or somebody make something to eat around this place?" Jack didn't care where it came from as long as it was grilled or fried.

"Of course," Syman nodded. "I will show you the Janari."

Syman

"Janari … that sounds promising." Jack stood and rubbed his stomach.

"Are you ever *not* hungry?" Nick mumbled.

Jack was relieved to hear his friend's voice and knew that he was going to be okay. "Nope," he paused. "Well, maybe when we were in that mine about to die, but after we were transported here … I was pretty much hungry again."

Nick made a sound that resembled a laugh, but Syman did not respond. Neither did Ilea. She was too busy trying to understand Syman's explanation of the Maker.

Syman took two bags from a hook by the door. One was simple cloth, but the other was tied at the top and heavier, slicker as if it had been dipped in wax. "If you will follow me," Syman directed Jack, then turned and walked out of the cave.

Jack had the distinct feeling that Syman didn't care if he came with him or not. But Jack was hungry, so he followed. Ilea was worried about Nick, so she sat down beside him. Gently, she returned his glasses to their proper place then began stroking his hair and humming softly.

Syman led Jack across the open platform, past the round open-sided room, past cut out entrances to other homes, past strangely put together people watching from within many of the doorways. They walked to the end of the platform. A place where the flat surface ended with smooth cut, sheer cliffs. Mountain walls that shot up straight out of the ground and blocked the pathway except for two wide openings. Three or four men could have lain across the width of each opening then stood on each other's shoulders and still not have reached the top. One opening led upward, with daylight shimmering across its stone, but the other disappeared into the dark depths of the mountain. This was the opening Syman chose. Jack thought about the mine in the desert where they had been trapped and almost died, and for a heartbeat, he hesitated. But his stomach won out and he followed Syman into the cave.

Several feet inside, Syman descended the massive stairs that led deeper into the mountain. Steps as wide as the cave opening and deep enough that Jack had to take three steps across before moving down onto the next step. This place was not worn by water or wind but cut smooth by a tool more powerful than Jack had ever seen.

As they continued deeper into the cave, Jack expected the light to fade, but instead they were surround by a warm glow that grew stronger the farther they went. Jack could look to either side and watch a mirrored version of himself and Syman descending into the depths of the cave. The reflected lights and images made the room feel as if it went on forever. White diamond-like rocks sparkled from the walls and steps. Just a few, here and there, but growing in number as they walked until great patches of white covered most of the steps and upper walls. Thin vines appeared along the edges where the steps met the walls. Lush green vines that became thicker as the white rocks increased in number. Jack was certain he could hear those vines singing or at least humming some erratic tune.

"The Makers put the crystals here," Syman explained, "so that we could live. The crystals make water and give life. He taught me to care for the plants and make food."

He led Jack deeper and deeper into the mountain until the walls opened outward and the ceiling rose two or three buildings high. A domed ceiling covered with crystals shining like a sun inside the mountain. The walls now contained crystals of different colors. Most were white, but red and blue and yellow crystals appeared in random patches along the lower walls. Shallow ruts carried water in river-like fashion along the edges of the room. Water dripped from the ceiling and trickled down the walls to find its way into the rivers. Plants grew in rows on shallow shelves that had been cut into the walls, just like the steps. Long narrow troughs held the plants on the shelves and in places along the ground. The stone was smooth cut with sharp right angles. Each shelf and each trough identical to the one before, but the plants varied. Deep green and pale, yellow leaves, spotted black ivies, and pink and blue berries hung from the walls. Patches of dark soil held what could have been broccoli or lettuce. Bushes held yellow and red tomato-like fruit. At least that's what it looked like. Jack had never watched broccoli or tomatoes grow and avoided eating them if possible. Nick would know what they were. He slipped out his camera and took a few pictures to show him when they went back.

As they walked, the cave became a forest. Tall broad-leaf trees held fruit Jack didn't recognize. And the leaves were not all green. Some were red and yellow and some even sparkled like the cave walls. The roots crawled across the top of the ground dipping into the rivers that wound between everything.

"As you can see, all that we need is here." Syman swept his hand toward the trees. "The Sericum plant grows in multiple colors. Their fibers are used to make our clothes and flooring and pillows." He turned to look at Jack. "Everyone has a skill taught to them by their parent. Weaving, cooking, growing ... we all share and work together for the benefit of all. No one is without. You may take what you need."

Syman

Jack stared in bewilderment, afraid he would never see another french fry or hamburger again.

"Deeper into the cave are the ore deposits. We have skilled workers who forge our tools and weapons if needed."

"So, are you in charge here?" Jack questioned, concerned about the whole sharing thing. In his experience, sharing typically meant I-get-a-lot-and-you-get-a-little-bit.

"I am the oldest here, but we have a council who meet and govern."

Jack nodded, still suspicious. "So, I can take whatever I want from this place?"

"You are our guest for now."

For now, Jack thought, *for now sounds funny.* He could feel his stomach rumble. "I don't suppose you have any meat?"

Syman handed Jack the wax covered bag and pointed to a pool of water where the ceiling dripped. "Fill this bag with water and I will gather food."

So, I guess there's no meat. "Okay ... whatever." Jack loosened the waxy bag and walked over to the pool. He knelt down and dipped the bag into the water, watching it fill. *I bet I could drink this whole thing by myself.*

He tightened the loops at the top and stood to watch Syman meandering among the bushes and trees filling his bag with fruit of various colors.

"Bananas?" Jack said, hoping there was something in this room he recognized. "All this grocery shopping is making me even hungrier," he mumbled.

Syman paused, tilted his head, then shook his head no. "Come," he said and led Jack past the bushes and trees.

The plants were thin here, but against the cave wall were long poles hung horizontally in racks with what looked like strips of meat wrapped and dangling from each rod. Smoke floated up from beneath the racks. Smoke from grassy-looking plants that did not burn. Misty, sweet smelling smoke that bathed the meat then dissipated without filling the cave.

"Meat," Syman pointed, then picked up a waxy piece of cloth from a pile on the ground. He took a smooth, hooked pole from against the wall then used it to pull several pieces of meat from the rack. He wrapped them inside the cloth, leaned the pole back against the wall, then placed the cloth inside the bag.

Jack tried to image what kind of animal had been sliced into the long strings of meat. "Snake," he mumbled. "Snake bacon. Just my luck."

Syman

Syman put the bag over his shoulder then led the way out of the cave. Jack grabbed an apple-looking fruit from a tree as they passed. He polished it on his shirt then took a bite. A honey flavor filled his mouth as juice dripped down his chin. *Maybe this place is not all bad.* Jack wiped his hand on his pants and followed Syman past the trees and viney walls back to the wide steps that led out of the cave. He took long, fast paced steps, so Jack had a hard time keeping up.

"Do you ever fly your food home?" Jack asked, imagining a dragon carrying a grocery bag.

"Sometimes. The dragon, as you call him, is a useful tool, but I am limited by size. Mass is finite."

"Mass... that's your weight ... sort of ... Nick taught me that. Maybe you could be a grizzly," Jack smirked. "Just a really short grizzly."

Syman ignored him.

At Syman's house, they found Ilea still sitting on the bench beside Nick. His wrist showed no signs of ever being injured. His face, however, was still pale.

"We brought dinner," Jack grinned. Both men carried in their supplies and laid then on the table by the firepit. "You should see their grocery store."

Syman

"There is food for everyone thanks to the Maker." Syman looked at Nick and Ilea. "I see your friend is feeling better."

Nick studied Syman. "You were the dragon?"

"Yes, but I am Syman as well."

Jack frowned at Nick, who was still pale from blood loss. "Hey buddy, what's the last thing you remember?"

Nick took a deep breath and sat up. "I remember being chased. Those men ... in cars ... Jack driving in the dark ... bumps and ..."

"I think you mean Jack's expert driving that saved your life." Jack stiffened his back to look more official.

"Yes ...that's what I meant." Nick offered a weak smile.

"The light?" Ilea did her best to speak in his language. "You remember?"

"You made the light, didn't you?" Jack didn't quite understand how it happened.

"We hid in the mine but there was no way out." Nick turned to look at Ilea. "Your bracelet was glowing and mine too. You made them glow. Somehow they connected … you made them connect to form the gateway."

"The light that brought us here … right?" Jack tried to help him remember.

"Yes," Nick agreed. "Ilea made the gateway that brought us here."

"And I carried you through and saved your lives … ta da!" Jack took a bow.

Syman walked over to Nick and Ilea then reached down to examine their bracelets. He lifted Ilea's wrist. "Your control band contains a white crystal shard and a partially functioning Sulston."

"SolStone," Ilea murmured, remembering the stories about the magic stone and its powers.

Syman glanced over at Nick's wrist and his beads. "The beads of your bracelet are crystals as well. Their colors are mixed. This could explain the increase in functionality."

"Increased functionality," Nick mused. "So, what is the functionality of her wristband?"

Syman lifted his head to stand straight. "Her bracelet regulates her body temperature." He tilted his head sideways in thought. "It also has the ability to open short transport windows for extended movement."

Ilea squinted in confusion while Nick's mind jumped with possibilities. *A short transport window ... is that like the window that brought us here? How far is short? And why doesn't Ilea understand her own bracelet?*

Syman returned to the table to open his bag and lay out the food he had collected. "You should eat. You need to regain your strength." He spoke to Nick as he worked.

Nick wasn't thinking about food. "Where did you get your bracelet?" He waited for Ilea to answer, but she just shrugged.

Ilea touched her wristband. "My father?"

Syman closed the cloth bag on the table. "The Maker created that device for the Tal. They could not maintain their body temperature."

"But you said she could use it to travel." Nick tried to stand, but he was still weak from blood loss.

Syman carried three round, yellow colored fruit over to his visitors. "Please eat. This will help restore your strength."

Everyone stared at Syman, not sure what to do next.

Syman

"Take ... a ... bite," Syman encouraged. "Gooooood." He drew out his words as though speaking to a child.

Nick took a bite and scowled at the bitterness of the fruit's skin. The flesh inside, however, was sticky sweet. This fruit held one large seed, like a peach or avocado except the seed was red. Nick tried to think of any food he had ever seen on Earth with a red seed. Nick took another bite, and Ilea giggled as the juice ran down his chin. He could already feel the effects of the fruit. His heartrate increased and his thinking cleared, much like the boost from a strong cup of coffee.

"I want to try some of that snake bacon." Jack put his yellow fruit back on the table and opened the waxy cloth that held the smoked meat. "A plant cooked this, Nick. You should see all the crazy plants growing underneath this mountain." He pulled out the waxed cloth and unwrapped the meat.

"Meat smoked by a plant," Nick shook his head. The color had returned to his face and he was feeling stronger. "Just exactly where are we?"

Syman moved beside the table where Jack was trying to break off a piece of the stringy meat. "You are in the Lost City on Regar," Syman answered Nick's question as if traveling to other worlds was a common occurrence. From beneath the table, he pulled out several thin, glassy bowls and cups. More work from the artisans of the city. "Please eat. You each need your strength."

Jack stretched his piece of meat until it snapped like rubber. "Sorry, Nick. You probably didn't hear all that about the City of the Lost becoming the Lost City. Guess it's like texting or something. The name got shorter, but that's where we are. Regar … Lost City." He took the smaller piece and bit into it, chewing, and tearing, and grinding his teeth into the meat. It tasted of the sweet smoke from the cave. "It's like wubbery jeky." Jack tried to describe the taste with a full mouth.

"Wubbery?" Nick mocked. "Maybe I'll skip the snake bacon."

Ilea walked to the table and filled a bowl with various foods, then returned to sit by Nick and offered to share. He tried a long red cucumber-looking fruit and some round, purple berries. Each time he took a bite, Nick held the food in his mouth analyzing its texture and taste, comparing it to those of Earth. The purple berries tasted oily, and he wondered if they were filled with proteins. The snake bacon was the only meat Jack had mentioned, and he was the best qualified to find meat in this place. Protein, vitamins, maybe these people didn't need any of those things. Nick still wasn't sure where they were. *Was this another planet or a parallel dimension? Did they come through an Einstein-Rosen bridge? Was Earth light years away or just on the other side of that wall?*

"How did you get here?" Ilea asked, listening to the millions of separate lifesongs singing inside of Syman.

"Here?" Syman didn't understand.

"So far away from the red moon."

Syman tilted his head sideways and his expression grew blank. Then, as if a switch had been thrown, his head righted and he began to speak. "You must come from the farthest side of the planet where the red moon is high in the sky." He mixed his words with Tal and English.

Nick looked up. *Planet ... Syman had said planet. We must be on another planet. That is the only explanation that makes sense.*

Ilea nodded. "My people are protected by the red moon."

Syman almost smiled. "I do not believe that protect is the correct term, but I understand the implication. I have lived on both sides of Regar. I was made close to your city of Luz, but the Maker brought me to this side of the planet."

Ilea did not understand this word *planet*. Maybe it was just his way of saying place or land. Either way, the red moon was on the other side. She had seen the edge of her moon on the horizon, so it must be true.

"Can you take me home?" Ilea said, then looked down at the ground to hide the sadness in her eyes. *I should be more grateful for this man's kindness. He has taken us in ... taken in strangers. I don't think my family would have done the same.* "I want to go home and see my brother and my mother." She wanted to see her father too, but in her heart, she knew he was dead. He could never have survived the wounds he received at the crystal mines. She should have been able to save him. *Why couldn't I save him?*

Syman looked at Ilea. "Your home is the mountain city of Luz ... correct?"

"Yes," Ilea looked in the dragon-man's green eyes. *Were they always green?* "Can you take us there?" With food and water, she could make the trek easily, but she couldn't carry Nick and Jack. And, she wasn't leaving without them.

"I can take you," Syman agreed. "But there are others here who will wish to travel with us. It will take time to make arrangements."

Syman

Nick was feeling stronger and couldn't resist a chance to find out more. "So, there are other people like Ilea living here?"

"No," Syman shook his head. "She is the only Tal in the city. But … there are other ground dwellers who may be anxious to return to the land beneath the red moon." He turned and walked out the doorway into the open courtyard.

"Byyyyeeee," Jack said, still chewing on a mouthful of snake bacon. "Guess he doesn't say goooooby."

Nick stood, still weak from blood loss, and walked over to pick up a piece of Jack's bacon. "What do you think about this guy?"

Jack swallowed. "You need to ask him about Jaika."

Nick nodded. "This could be her world, but I don't think this is her city. She said her father was a king … remember?"

Jack gritted his teeth, still chewing. "This is like gum … do you think she was telling the truth?"

"I do," Nick paused, "at least the truth as she remembered. Some kids just think their father is a king."

"Mine sure wasn't," Jack mumbled. "Still, it's hard to pretend your house is a castle."

"Maybe I just wanted it to be true because she did."

Jack grinned. "Ilea ... does Jaika live here?" He shouted the words across the room to help her understand.

Ilea stood and moved closer to her two friends. "Jaika?" She thought about the little girl she had met in the forest. The little girl she had given the beaded bracelet to ... the bracelet that Nick now wore. Then she shook her head no. "Red moon."

Nick did his best to understand. "So, she lives by the red moon?"

"When you were dying outside, I saw a piece of a red moon just above the horizon." Jack stretched a new piece of snake bacon."

"When I was dying ... nice to hear."

Jack rolled his eyes. "We didn't let you die. Ilea saved you."

"So, you saw a red moon?" Nick tried to keep Jack focused.

"Yeah, behind us … or in front depending on which way you're facing." He broke off another bite of bacon.

Nick shook his head at his friend's insatiable hunger. "So, Ilea … you and Jaika live under the red moon?"

Ilea nodded. She didn't know how to explain that her city was in the mountains and Jaika's was full of ground dwellers, but it didn't seem to matter. If they could just travel closer to the red moon, that would be enough. She could show them Palon and the mountains of Luz.

"Even if Jaika's dad is not a king, we need to find her." Jack seemed confident that it would happen, that they would find her alive and safe. "Maybe we should ask Syman. He could tell us who's president … and where the red moon is."

Nick studied Ilea as they spoke, wondering just how much she understood. "You are right, Jack. That's what we need to do."

"We need to find a city of blue people. And a city of not-blue people with a king. That should be easy enough." Jack smiled as if he had just solved all their problems.

Syman

Nick smiled. He never thought they would get this far. Ilea had brought them through a doorway of light to another world. That should be the most difficult part. So, finding Jaika now should be easy.

"I just want to go home." Ilea tried hard to make them understand. She just wanted to see her mother and Dodgen. She didn't want to save anyone else, she just wanted to fly beneath the red moon and see her home again.

Nick slipped his arm around her shoulder. "I would like to see your home, too."

"What the … ?" Jack stared past his friends in disbelief. "Who is that?"

Syman had retuned, but he was not alone. Beyond Syman, in the stone doorway, Nick could see a woman standing with a creature behind her who was twice her size. "Is that a centaur?" was all Nick could think to say.

"What's a centaur?" Jack mused as he turned to study the front door.

"From mythology," Nick tried to explain, but couldn't find the words.

As the woman stepped through the stone doorway, the man … the creature … followed. True to the stories of mythology, his torso was human while his lower body had four legs and was covered in shaggy fur. A horse, but not quite. His golden hair hung long in a braid down his back. His powerful arms held two handles of a woven laundry-size basket. But his legs, his legs were far from human. They shifted beneath him as he walked. Strong legs covered with thick, almost black fur. Wide feet with three webbed toes much like a camel. As least, that was Nick's assessment.

"A centaur ... but a camel, not a horse," Nick hadn't meant to speak out loud.

"I do not know this word ... centaur." Syman wrinkled his nose and then turned to speak with his visitors in their own language. He switched his words back and forth from language to language, translating when he felt it was needed. "Zaldi is a hybrid created by the Maker."

"Of course he is," Nick shook his head hard to clear his thoughts.

The woman wore a shapeless, poncho-style covering and carried a rolled, sleeping mat held tight against her right side. As she greeted Syman, she raised her right arm to pat him on the shoulder, but the sleeping mat did not move. Her dress rippled as they spoke, and it took Jack several minutes to understand that the arm on Syman's shoulder was not connected to the arms holding the mat.

Syman

"She has three arms," Jack smiled, feeling as though he was the only one in the room who noticed.

"On the contrary," Syman correct, "Ciya has six."

He spoke to her in some strange language and she raised all six arms. They extended through the folds of her dress.

"That is amazing," Nick stepped forward and offered his hand to shake.

Ciya shook his hand and patted his head with still another hand. Then she laughed at the shocked look on his face. She turned away from Nick to speak once again with Syman. Her language was strange, but she laughed and smiled and chattered like a bird making everyone feel welcome. Zaldi knelt on his front legs to set down the basket, while Ciya pointed and explained the contents. Her arms moved in multiple directions, waving at Nick and Jack and the basket and the mat, all at the same time. She bowed then shouted to someone outside the door. A young bare-chested boy with four arms ran inside to speak with Syman, giggling and fidgeting just like any elementary-school boy from Earth, except for the additional arms.

Ilea sat back down on the bench trying to melt into the shadows. She had heard stories of such creatures. Amazing creatures that did not look like anything or anyone else living beneath the red moon. The stories were always full of death and cruelty, but she felt none of these things inside this woman or her son. Still, they would have to be careful with these strangers. "Thank you," she mumbled, but no one heard.

Nick watched in awe, stunned not only by the visitors' strange appearances but by their kindness. Syman had taken them into his home. This woman and centaur had brought food and blankets to people they didn't even know. Nick could have been a murderer, but they didn't seem to care.

"Does everyone here look different?" Jack sat down on the bench beside the table, unaffected by the events in the room. "You know, different than me?"

Syman nodded. "We were each designed by the Maker to be unique. Their ancestors were brought here to live under my care. Ciya is the sixth generation in her family. Zaldi is only fourth. Longevity varies among each species, but I have seen all of them."

"All of them?" Nick repeated.

"Ciya," a woman's voice called from outside.

Nick watched as a phosphorescent-skinned woman paused in the doorway. Pale green, her skin glowed where it peeked out from her loose-fitting tunic, just like the undersea creatures Nick had read about in school. Her arms and legs were bare and shimmered even though it was light outside. Darker green lines wove along her hands and places on her arms, penciled lines that Nick thought might be veins. A rope-belt tied the dress at her tiny waist making her body look willowy thin. Nick was certain she was much younger than Ciya. Her hair was blue-green and seemed speckled with glitter. Patchy spots of leafy greens that sparkled here and there. She smiled as she entered, and she too carried a basket.

"Mmmmm," Jack's mouth watered from the warm smell of bread coming from her basket. "No more snake bacon," he muttered to himself. *I like her already.*

"Luna," she announced, holding her hand to her chest and lowering her head.

Syman mimicked her greeting with a quick bow. "Her mother was with me from the beginning. Luna is seventh generation Regarian."

"Regarian," Nick puzzled. So many new creatures, so many new words. He would never keep up.

Syman lifted the cloth that covered the basket to reveal long loaves of bread, like the french bread Jack ate at the Italian place by his dorm. "Luna is one of our bread makers." Syman explained. "She is quite skilled. She often fuses the dough with fruit or sweets or spices you may have never tried."

Jack shuttered. "So, they have fruitcake is this place too."

Nick smiled and snickered, then looked away not wanting to hurt anyone's feelings.

Syman tilted his head sideways in his familiar thinking stance, but only for an instant. "Your words fruit and cake are not accurate. The texture of bread is heavier than cake, and the sweet content …"

"It's okay. It's okay," Jack interrupted. "I was trying to be funny."

"I understand," Syman replied.

He said he understood, but Jack didn't think so. Then Syman looked at Luna and said something that made her laugh.

Jack turned to Ilea, who looked small against the back wall. "Help me, Ilea. What did he say?"

She couldn't help but smile. "Something about you being so hungry you can't tell which food is which."

"It's not funny, but it's probably true," Jack sighed. "I don't want any more snake bacon." He rubbed his stomach and everyone in the room could hear it grumble.

"It will be night soon," Syman repeated this phrase in several languages.

Nick bowed to Ciya and Luna, trying to find a way to say thank you.

"Yeah," Jack said. "Thanks for your help."

Zaldi backed out of the house then spun and knelt close to the doorway. Luna and Ciya and her son climbed on his back. He pushed up from the ground and walked away as if he carried nothing at all.

"Mmmmm …he must be really strong," Jack was talking about Zaldi but looking at Luna's breadbasket. "Sure smells good," he sniffed.

Syman sniffed as well. "I believe a bath is in order."

"Huh?" Jack shrugged.

"I think he just said we stink," Nick sniffed as well. "We have been through a lot."

"Smells fine to me." Jack winked at Ilea.

"It is late," Syman explained. "I will show you the water rooms in the morning."

Syman

Syman busied himself making pallets on the floor. Once he was finished, he nodded and said, "Sleep well. I will see you in the morning." Then he unhooked a curtain that dropped across a closet-sized room beside the kitchen and disappeared inside.

"Guess it's bedtime," Jack wrapped up the rest of the snake bacon then tore off a large piece of Luna's bread.

Nick watched the crumbs dropping from his friend's mouth. "So, tomorrow we find out how to travel to the red moon." He yawned and shook his head at his Jack's insatiable appetite. Then he stretched out on one of the pallets.

"Sounds good." Jack agreed, stuffing the rest of his bread into his mouth. He laid down on a blanket beside the cushioned bench where Ilea sat.

Ilea pulled her feet up to lay down on the bench, glad she was not alone in such a strange place. "The red moon," she whispered. *I'm going home.*

Newcomers

Nick sat up trying to remember where he was and why there was a gong ringing outside. Jack rubbed his eyes and stretched as Syman walked past him out into the courtyard. Nick got up and followed him as far as the doorway then peered out like a child into the courtyard from the edge of the opening. People of all ages and appearances met in the open gazebo-type building in the middle. They chanted in unison, greeted each other, then went their separate ways.

"I don't think they are killing children or anything like that." Jack sat up and his stomach grumbled.

Ilea stood and flexed her wings open and shut several times.

"That is amazing ... you have to admit ... that is truly amazing." Jack watched Ilea stretching and then stood up and headed for the food still sitting out on the table.

Syman

Nick turned to see Ilea folding up her wings, and Syman walked past him, returning from the chant-session outside. "So, does the gong mean to come outside?"

Syman stopped. "This tradition was established by the Maker. We give our thanks to Gelquin and to each other for having a safe place to live, enough to eat … being cared for. We do this each morning."

"Gelquin," Ilea repeated.

"Gelquin made all things so that my Maker could make me." Syman seemed unconcerned with Nick's curiosity.

"Make, make, make… something is wrong with that statement." Nick pushed his glasses up to rub the bridge of his nose. "Who made what?"

Syman tilted his head to the side, and his face relaxed without expression. Then he straightened, and the brightness returned to his eyes.

Nick huffed. "Make … Maker … Creator … it's all the same isn't it?"

"You must eat and then I will explain further." Syman sat down on the wide bench against the wall to wait. His head tilted slightly sideways. His eyes dim.

Syman

"This feels weird," Jack whispered, but didn't stop eating.

Ilea and Nick took some bread and fruit from the table. They watched each other as they ate, feeling Syman's stare. "Weird ... yes," Nick agreed. *Why doesn't he eat with us?*

After a few minutes, Syman's eyes brightened and he stood. "I have the solution. Come with me," he announced, putting an end to breakfast. Then he walked past them to lead the way out the door and back to the stone ramps they had climbed when they entered the Lost City. Nick, Jack, and Ilea followed close behind.

Nick studied the walls and the glowing lights of the columns in the tunnel. He had only hazy memories of this place. Jack had carried him up the ramp and into Syman's house. The lights and the stone were just a big blur from the day before.

At the end of the ramp, they could see the endless sand beneath the yellow sun. Syman stretched out his hands as if to encompass the whole land. "Gelquin made the sun and the stars and both moons. He made the sand and even the stones which bond together to make the mountain. But my Maker created the Janari. My Maker cut our homes from the rock and he made us." Syman looked over his shoulder at Nick as though he was expecting a thank you for answering the question.

Nick scratched his head. "Us ... you mean ..."

"I will clarify," Syman continued. "He made me as well as the first of each species. The originals have all died, but I continue to protect their descendants."

"So, you are really old?" Jack snickered.

"I have specific regenerative properties which allow me to continue."

Nick was beginning to understand. These people had multiple gods, just like many of the past civilizations on Earth. One god made the sand here while another made the people. This setup seemed logical. "Gelquin made the land, and the Maker created the people and your city."

"Yes," Syman agreed, then spoke in the Tal language. "Now that I have clarified, I will show you the water rooms."

Syman had been speaking in English, so Ilea didn't understand most of his explanation. But then, Gelquin didn't need an explanation. She already understood who the creator of all things was and why they would worship him.

Syman

Syman turned and walked past the others and back up the stone ramp.

Jack sneered. "He seems so cold ... so ..."

"Robotic?" Nick finished his sentence.

They stared at each other, hypnotized by the possibilities.

"Wow! A robot ... that makes complete sense. Just like the robots on TV who can transform." Jack turned to follow Syman. "Come on. He might do something strange. We don't want to miss it."

Ilea looked at Nick to see if she should follow this odd man with so many lifesongs. Nick nodded his approval and they made their way back into the Lost City. Syman walked up the ramp and through the open courtyard retracing the path he had taken when he led Jack to the Janari, except this time they did not follow the steps all the way down. Once through the entrance, they followed a sharp right turn to enter a narrow passageway that ended in a cave dripping with vines and water. As they entered, Ilea could see a massive, round pool cut into the stone, filled with water that bubbled up in the middle. Red and yellow vines climbed the walls and draped from the ceiling making curtain-like doorways around the room.

Ilea climbed into the pool of water sinking up to her waist. She spread her wings and then submerged beneath the crystal-clear water. Jack kept waiting for someone to say something, or do something, but they just stood there, watching her wings floating on top of the water. Just as he decided she needed to be rescued, Ilea burst from beneath the water. Her wings striking the water as she rose. She twisted and fluttered and giggled. Her hair hung in her eyes and her clothes looked painted on her skin. Then she shook. Her wings, her hair, her arms, she shook her body sending water spraying across the room.

"I hope that wasn't the drinking water." Jack couldn't picture himself bathing in a bathtub with Ilea.

"You can use the main pool with Ilea or the more private rooms along the walls." He handed the basket to Nick. "You will need these clean clothes."

"Thanks," Nick mumbled. He wasn't about to take off his clothes in front of Syman or Ilea.

Jack walked toward the back of the room still watching Ilea enjoying the water. *My little bird in a birdbath.* He lifted the vines to pass beneath. "Hey, Nick, come look. It's a shower."

Nick glanced over at Syman then joined Jack at the back of the room. He passed beneath the vines to see his friend pulling on a chain that released a stream of water. The vines acted as partitions creating four private rooms along the cave wall with each room having a chain.

"It's warm." Jack's eyes were wide in surprise as he pulled on the chain. "How do they make it warm?"

Nick studied the round opening in the stone where the water was released. The wall beneath it was rich with white crystals. "I'm not sure," he answered, not willing to try and explain his current working theory of the crystals in the walls. "But I brought you some clothes." He held up the basket.

"Alien clothes! Niiiice." Jack walked over and dug in the basket, pulling out several tunics and soft pants. "I'm taking the big ones, okay? Don't we need a towel?"

Nick smiled at his friend. He could always find the good in every situation. "Stand next to the white crystals in the wall after your clean. I have a feeling it might be helpful." Jack nodded and took his clothes.

Nick exited through the vines to find a shower-room of his own. After finding a dry place to stash the basket, he disrobed and pulled on the chain. The water was indeed warm. He stood beneath it feeling the sand and sweat wash away. The water left him, not only clean, but refreshed and invigorated. Nick released the chain and did as he had instructed Jack and stood by the wall peppered with white crystals. His skin dried quickly so he was able to put on the tunic and pants. He had to roll up the waist to keep the legs from dragging on the ground. Jack started singing then appeared through the vines.

"Is that your college fight song?" Nick asked, shaking his head at Jack's clothes. His pants were too short, and his tunic stretched tight across his chest and back.

"Yeah. Guess I'm out of the game for this season so I thought I'd get in a fight song. Man, that water made me feel good!"

Nick knew it had something to do with the crystals. Energy transfer maybe, but he wasn't sure. "Where's Ilea?" Nick asked as they joined Syman by the pool.

"She is outside drying off." Syman replied, turning to lead them out of the bathing room.

Jack shuddered. "This guy is creepy sometimes. Like a ..."

"Machine," Nick finished, raising his eyebrows as if to say I-told-you-so.

"Oh, yeah. I forgot."

Syman

They carried their dirty clothes and followed Syman up the ramp and out into the morning sunlight. Ilea spun and dove and landed just in front of them. Her clothes were dry, almost, but her hair had come loose from its bands and stuck out in scattered directions. She didn't seem to mind. Nick wondered if the water had made her feel as energized as it did him. She shook her wings then closed them into a cape that fell behind her. Its thin white bones hooking over her shoulders.

"Now I need your help." Syman looked at Ilea unconcerned with her appearance. "I need your healing skills."

"If you guys are leaving," Jack grinned, "can I take Nick back inside? I want to show him the food room."

"The Janari is open to everyone," Syman explained.

"So that's aaaa yes?" Jack wondered if Syman could laugh or tell a joke.

"Yes," Nick answered instead. "But I don't like the idea of being separated from Ilea."

"Have you seen her claws?" Jack didn't think there was anyone here she couldn't stop.

Syman

Ilea understood enough of the conversation to see Nick's concern. "I will help Syman. I will be safe." She patted Nick on the shoulder in reassurance and then turned to Syman for instructions.

Jack took Nick to the Janari, and Syman led Ilea up the ramp beside the Janari to the next level with more carved-out cave- like homes that lined the cliffs. This level looked much like the one before, and Ilea wondered just how many levels of homes existed in this city.

"Sanar!" Syman called out to one of the many entrances.

A woman appeared in the stone doorway. A woman with caramel-colored skin and long, tawny hair that curled in every direction. Her eyes glowed like the sun. She wore a thin skirt that clung to her legs and almost touched the ground. Her top had thin straps and was short enough to reveal the images painted across her stomach. Drawings of the red moon and the sun and a long thin creature that coiled and slithered like the one that had lived in Mig's shed back on Earth. Her lifesong, however, drew Ilea's attention more than her appearance. Her lifesong rose and fell in joy and anger, creating chaos and disorder as though two very different people lived inside her.

"I'm here," the woman sighed.

Syman nodded in greeting. "May we visit the newcomer?"

"Of course," her eyes flashed with yellow light. "He is," she growled and showed her spiked teeth, "better." Her eyes softened as she looked past Syman to Ilea. "Who are you bringing into my house?"

"She is Tal."

"I see that. Why is she here?"

Syman pointed behind him. "Ilea is also a newcomer." Then he pointed back to the woman in the doorway. "She is Sanar. Sanar is our healer." Syman continued to explain as they entered. "Ilea is a healer as well."

Sanar smiled at Ilea's water-blue eyes. "So, you are a healer." Her soft voice had returned, and she spoke in the language of Palon. The yellow of her eyes softened as well.

Ilea nodded. She couldn't remember ever seeing anyone with yellow skin and hair. *Why do we not have people like her in Palon? Why do we not have any of these people in Palon?*

As they stepped inside, Ilea could see that the main room was used for cooking with stacked shelves of colored bottles and baskets of plants. The strong smells bathed her skin and dripped from the walls.

Syman

Syman led the way into a separate room carved deeper into the mountain. In this room, a man slept on a pallet on the floor. Parts of his body were wrapped in a colorful blanket. One of his eyes was protected with a dark cloth. Ilea could feel the hunks of flesh torn away along his left arm and leg even though they were covered with bandages. His leg was twisted at the knee and ankle in directions that bones should never go.

"This man was carried to us by the Breen. Sanar has cared for him as best she could."

Ilea listened to his lifesong though it was dulled with sleep. There was something familiar about this ground dweller. She had seen this man before. Each creature has a unique lifesong that stays with her memory even after just one meeting, but it was hard to be sure with this man. His lifesong screamed with pain and the grogginess of tonic or oils or some other concoction used to dull the pain. Either way, she didn't want to be near him. A darkness ... somewhere inside him ... fought its way out past the sleep and the pain. A darkness she had seen before ... somewhere.

Sanar watched Ilea from the doorway. "There is not much left of this man. I could use your help. Perhaps your skills are greater than mine."

Ilea didn't want to help him. She didn't even want to be in this room with him. But these people had been so kind, she didn't want to say no. "I will try," she murmured, wishing there was another way.

Ilea stepped closer to the pallet, closer to the ground dweller, and let her lifesong whisper across his, searching for parts that could be healed but keeping her song close and safe. "Pieces of his lifesong ... his body ... are gone. His eye, his knee ... I cannot repair such damage."

"But some repairs can be made ... correct?" Syman asked.

"Yes. I can make him better, but not whole." Ilea could see the scars laced throughout his body from Sanar's work. She had kept him alive.

"Understand?" Sanar spoke to the man on the pallet even though he couldn't hear. "She can help you heal so that you can see your son again."

"So, he wants to see his son. Good ... that will give him a reason to live ... a reason to fight." Ilea hoped her words sounded sincere. Her lifesong quivered at the thought of connecting with his darkness. She moved closer to the pallet and dropped to her knees to be near the stranger. Sitting child-like beside him, she lowered her head and reached out to touch his skin. As she moved, she hummed, letting her lifesong nudge the edge of his. The man gasped and raised his chest from the mat. Even unconscious, his body was so frail and sensitive, he felt pain as Ilea's lifesong entered his own.

There were long scars where Sanar had healed his stomach and the bones in his back. His most important parts seemed to be working, even with the scars, so Ilea decided to try and help with the pain. She closed her eyes and coaxed the gashes beneath the bandages on his arm to begin closing, at least enough to dull the ache. With each touch, with each movement, Ilea could feel the darkness in this man. It whispered to her as she worked, scratching at her lifesong.

Sanar quieted her mind to feel Ilea working, pulling her song into her own, allowing Ilea's lifesong to bring her peace. "Can you feel it?" Sanar spoke in the Tal language, watching Ilea's response. "The gray ... *the night?*"

How does she know my language? Ilea kept her eyes closed and fought to stay focused. "Yes," she breathed, "it is strong."

Her song shifted to his knee. Parts of the bone were missing, torn away by something or someone with great strength. The joint did not have enough pieces to heal, so Ilea began the task of connecting his upper and lower leg. It would no longer bend, but it was preferable to removing it. As she worked, Sanar joined her, moving her lifesong deeper into this man to push back the darkness within him. Ilea trembled as this woman's song passed her own. It held the same darkness, the same torment as this man.

Ilea pulled back and looked up at Syman. "He will live in pain forever. His leg will ache and slow his walk."

"Maybe that's what he deserves." Sanar eyes shown bright yellow. "Not everyone deserves to live."

Ilea wasn't sure if Sanar spoke about this man or herself. "I am not the creator. I will not make that decision." She looked back at Syman. "I will need to come back tomorrow. His body cannot heal in one day."

"Yes," Syman nodded. "When he is healed, we will travel to your homes ... to Palon and Luz."

Ilea huffed. She did not want to wait for this man. She wanted to go home. She could leave on her own tomorrow and see her brother in just a few days. This waiting ... and helping ... was frustrating.

"He cannot eat. The food does not help. He will not grow stronger without food." Sanar interrupted. "I cannot repair ..." She searched for the words.

Ilea felt her despair and decided to try once more. Anything to increase her chances of getting home. She took a deep breath and sent her lifesong searching for wounds she had missed. So much of this man's body was damaged, it had been easy to pass over the tiny punctures in his organs. Tiny holes from a weapon or claw dotted the places in his body that held food and took away the poisons. She fought the heavy scars that had formed around the punctures. Thick scars that held the wounds open and could no longer heal.

Ilea growled low. "It is impossible. Scars cannot heal. I cannot …"

"He needs a new wound so that you can repair it." Sanar moved closer to Ilea, her skirt swirling around her legs as she moved.

Ilea frowned. She had never considered injuring a person to allow healing, but it may be the only way. Ilea raised her hand and wiggled her fingers toward Sanar.

"Together?" Sanar questioned, dropping to her knees opposite Ilea. The stranger between them.

They joined hands and lifesongs across his body. Ilea felt Sanar's lifesong rise within the man. Loud and strong, it tore at the scar tissue that formed along the holes in his body. Sanar did not sing. She growled low and breathed, blowing out her air and the yellow light that destroyed. Ilea's song came behind her destruction to begin the healing. The raw and bleeding pieces intertwined to become whole. The stranger writhed and twisted beneath the blanket. Even sedated, he could feel Sanar's destruction.

Syman stood fixed, motionless, never shifting his gaze or his balance. He watched and tried to understand. He stored away the sounds and sights into his memories.

Ilea pulled away, breathless. "I need to rest." She did not want to work on this man anymore.

Sanar stood and motioned for them to follow. Together, they walked into the cooking room to sit at a small table. In the center, Sanar placed a basket full of food wrapped in colored cloths. More cloth decorated the handle and sides of the basket, and it was easy to see that this had been meant as a gift.

"We will eat." Sanar offered.

"But this was a gift to you," Ilea resisted.

"Yes. I cannot heal as you can, but people are still grateful when I help. So now, you are helping me." Sanar's eyes had turned blue and gentle. Her skin was pale with bits of blue and green swirling inside the yellow.

For the first time since her arrival, Ilea saw Syman smile. The smile was practiced and empty. Even when smiling, he seemed to have no emotions, good or bad.

"I am pleased to see you so happy." Syman smiled at Sanar. She matched his smile as if they had practiced hundreds of times.

Sanar removed the food from the basket while she talked with Syman about past visitors. Ilea listened to the pieces of their conversation that she could understand and felt the joy in Sanar. It was clear Syman had spent many suns helping Sanar control her emotions. So many stories of people and disaster and adventure in a city Ilea never knew existed.

Their words quieted as the basket grew empty. When they could eat no more, Sanar stood and held out her hand to Ilea. They joined hands and returned to the stranger's side to continue.

Darkness

For three suns, Ilea and Syman returned to work with Sanar, but this morning, the man was awake. When they entered the back room, he was sitting up, leaning against a pillow and the stone wall. Sanar had fashioned him a proper eye-patch to replace the ragged cloth that had covered half of his face. His long, dark hair was greasy and hung in clumps down his cheeks and around his beard. She could feel the anger stirring in his lifesong. He ate from a small bowl on the floor beside him, picking at his food.

"He wishes to die," Sanar seethed, her eyes burned yellow. "I cannot convince him otherwise. He believes he must die for his crimes." She growled low and clenched her fingers in a fist.

Ilea looked at Syman. "What crimes?"

Syman ignored the anger brewing inside Sanar.

"Theft, murder, lies, cruelty ... actions taken against another." Sanar wanted them to know what dangers this man might hold for the city.

Syman

Ilea studied the man on the pallet. "So which of these crimes have you committed?"

He glared with his one eye then laughed. "Everything. Every crime you can think of, I have done it." Then he looked up at the ceiling like he was expecting someone to be there. "Haven't I."

Sanar shrieked, "Then you deserve to die!" She turned her back to the others and fought to balance her emotions.

"Her abilities are volatile and difficult to control. She will find balance." Syman could have explained her chemical system and the flaws in her design, but that was not relevant to the task at hand.

Ilea felt this woman's lifesong rise and fall and then quiet. Sanar turned back around. Her lifesong had softened, and her eyes dulled to gray. "I have kept this man alive, but now … now I am not sure we should have helped him."

Ilea stepped closer to the man, "Don't you want to see your son?"

The stranger looked down at his food and refused to answer.

"You are well enough. We will leave tomorrow," Syman told the stranger. "I have made preparations."

Syman

Ilea gasped. It was time. She could barely believe the words. The dragon-man was taking her home. "Tomorrow," Ilea repeated. She needed to hear the word again.

"We will travel at night, so you have this sun and the next to heal." Syman explained.

Ilea was anxious to go home, so she tried again. "No matter what you have done, don't you want to see your son again?"

The stranger looked up into her eyes. "Perhaps ... one last time."

"Then you will let me help you?" Ilea wanted to explain how hard she and Sanar had been working to keep him alive. She wanted to shout that they had been wasting their time and that she could have already been home ... that he was keeping her from her family. But instead, she filled her thoughts with memories. *Your gift is for everyone*, Adolphus had said. *I miss you father. Wherever you are ... I miss you.*

"You will find this easier if you lie down." Ilea wove her lifesong into the stranger as he shifted to lie flat on the pallet.

Sanar watched as Ilea sat beside the man on the pallet, never making a move to help her. Ilea would have to work alone today. If this man was guilty of such crimes, healing him … sending him back to his people seemed wrong, so Sanar would only watch.

Ilea waved one hand over the stranger's legs and stomach. The wounds inside him were quiet which allowed her to see past the scars and the pain to his true lifesong. Once she could see him completely, her insides twisted into knots. She shifted her legs and pulled away. *This cannot be*, she told herself. *Why is he here?* Her heart tightened as she moved both hands over his chest where his lifesong was strongest. Her song joined with his to find the true colors and movement and sound, looking … hoping … that what she saw was not the truth. Beyond his lifesong, she felt the hum of the shattered blue crystal he wore around his neck.

Her hands recoiled in disgust and Ilea scooted back toward the edge of the pallet. She stood and backed away. Her eyes wide with anger and fear. "Who are you?" she growled and flexed her claws. "You were there … in the courtyard … with the red-haired man. You were there when I flew from the prison … you and the blue light that sent me away."

The stranger sat up on the pallet fascinated by Ilea's water-blue eyes. "I am Oberon. And you … you are Seela's daughter."

Ilea growled low again. "What have you done to my mother?" She raised her claws as if to strike.

Syman

Syman stepped in front of her. "You will not ..."

Ilea stepped sideways to see past Syman. "I want the truth!"

"I did not hurt your mother," Oberon lied. "She came to Devant looking for you. I kept trying to find you, so your mother stayed. The SolStone ... I tried to make the stone bring you back. But ... I failed."

Ilea searched his lifesong for lies, but he was too angry for her to see clearly. His heart thundered in his chest. His blood boiled making his wounds screamed out in pain. He could be lying. He could be hiding the truth.

"Your mother helped me find my son," he tried to sound sincere. After all, it wasn't completely a lie.

Ilea's face softened. "So, my mother is safe?"

"She was in Devant when I was brought here, so she may be safe at home by now." Oberon lied again. He knew she was locked in his prison. She could be dead for all he knew.

"Why ... why did you send me away? And my brother ... what did you do to my brother?" Ilea shook with questions. Dodgen had been with her when this man used his magic to send her away.

Syman

"It was an accident." Oberon knew she could tear him apart if no one intervened. Maybe he didn't want to die after all, at least not this way. "The SolStone was too powerful, but your brother is safe. I know this to be true."

Ilea closed her eyes and tried to remember. "We had gone to the crystal mine ... those people were dying." Her heart ached at the memory of the faded lifesongs of the mine workers. "The soldiers took us ..." Ilea opened her eyes at the bitter memories. "They killed my father!" She growled and stepped forward.

Syman moved into her path again.

"The mines belonged to Kaleus. The red-haired man you spoke of. I had nothing to do with the mines. He put those prisoners there." Oberon had known about the prisoners but hadn't bothered to help them. "It doesn't matter anymore. The mines are closed ... the people are free." Oberon was telling the truth this time. "Merith saw to that." He could have told her about the soldiers and Jaika and the Breen who had destroyed his body and left him in the sand, but instead, he waited to see what she knew. "Forgive me," he whispered, feigning the guilt he knew he should feel.

Ilea wanted to believe him. She wanted to believe that her brother and mother were safe and that his man had not meant to hurt her.

Syman

Oberon needed her to believe him. He needed all of these strangers if he was ever going to see his son, Davin, again. He needed to explain. He needed to tell him that he had been wrong. Oberon no longer wanted to die.

"Will you continue to heal him?" Syman asked.

Ilea hesitated. She wanted to go home and Syman seemed to think this man needed to travel with them. For now, she would help, but just for now. "Yes," she mumbled. "I will continue."

She moved back to the pallet and sat down beside the man. Ilea laid her hands in her lap and opened her claws. She looked up into the stranger's one clear eye as she flexed them open and closed until she was certain he understood. "Who are you?" Ilea asked again.

"I am Oberon, once Guardian of the temple of Gelquin." He hoped she was a believer.

Ilea flexed her claws one last time as she reached out her hand to touch his knee. It was difficult to heal with so much hatred in her heart. She had to drive it away and think only of the shattered bones in his leg. The bones around his knee that had meshed together. There would be no bend here. The leg would be stiff and shorter than his other leg and never work as it did before. It would be difficult to walk, but he would have to make do. Somehow, that didn't bother Ilea. It was simply justice.

She let her lifesong flow across his chest and arms and up into the lifeless void that had been his eye. When she had finished, she stood. "You will never be whole," she explained, "Oberon, once Guardian of the temple."

He shook his head. "At least the pain is gone."

"Your leg," she pointed to his knee, "will never bend again. It will be lifeless and without pain."

"I understand."

"I will make arrangements so that he can be carried." Syman spoke up from behind Ilea.

"Good," she answered. She didn't want this man to slow them down.

Ilea looked at Sanar who had been watching in silence. She nodded and they both tried to smile. It felt good to have an ally, a friend, who could understand the joy and pain that came through healing others. Syman moved toward the door and Ilea followed. As they exited, Ilea turned and flexed her claws one last time at Oberon.

Tremor

Jack walked with Syman toward the Janari carrying cloth bags to hold the food they would carry on their trip to Ilea's home. Syman seemed to think they wouldn't need much, so Jack had tagged along to supervise. Being hungry in the desert didn't sound like much of a plan. He was not a genius, but food and water seemed like a really important part of a trip.

As they neared the doorway of the Janari, Jack felt the ground tremble beneath his tennis shoes. "Did you feel that?" Jack picked up his foot and looked beneath it for a bug or snake.

"The ground shifts from time to time." Syman continued walking.

"This is a mountain. It shouldn't move." Jack looked around him wondering if Syman knew what he was talking about.

As he lifted his foot to continue walking, the ground shook again. "That's not right!" Jack snarled at Syman, but he just kept walking.

Jack followed, but with each step toward the Janari, the trembling of the earth grew stronger. He stopped to look behind him. He could feel the ground shaking beneath his feet like a great train roaring past, but behind him, nothing seemed to be moving. The shaking was coming from inside the Janari.

"I'm not going down there." Jack shook his head and backed away. "Whatever's happening is happening in there." He pointed a quivering finger at the cave.

"You may be correct." Syman studied the doorway into the Janari.

The stone that framed the doorway twisted and the ground beneath it split. A jagged crack erupted from inside the Janari, opening the ground a hand's width between Jack and Syman. Behind Jack, another crack opened the ground to connect with the first one. A crooked 'x' carved into the mountain. The floor beneath Syman dropped. Only a few inches, but it was enough to drive them both to the ground to keep from falling.

Jack's fingers slid across the smooth ground without finding a hold. As he fought to try and stand, he watched the stone doorway into the Janari begin to crumble. Pieces rained to the ground. Dust filled the doorway, and Jack could hear the shouts from inside. The words were not in a language he knew, but there was no mistaking the cries for help. One final scream escaped as the doorway collapsed.

Jack looked up to see Syman standing and unshaken. "Who is inside?" Jack yelled.

"I don't know," Syman replied, "but we need to get them out."

"Duuuh," Jack huffed as he stood and dusted off his pants.

People began to slink out of their homes, taking slow cautious steps and waiting for the ground to shake again. Seeing Syman uninjured in the courtyard seemed to give them courage. They whispered in their strange languages. Jack felt like he was listening to chattering birds.

Syman shouted a word Jack did not understand, then began barking orders in multiple languages. The people scattered to return with ropes and harnesses and metal hooks that Jack knew would never pull those stones apart.

"I'm going to get Nick," Jack explained to Syman, who wasn't listening. But before he could leave, Nick and Ilea appeared among the crowd of people.

"What's happening?" Nick yelled over the shouts of the others.

"The ground is …" Ilea searched for the right word. "Breaking."

Jack hung his head. "I think we got that part."

Ilea didn't understand his sarcasm. She wanted to tell him that the ground was changing, evolving … dying, but she didn't know how.

Some of the stronger people were already working on the rocks that blocked the doorway. Driving hooks between the stones and tying off rope, they intended to pry loose the boulders.

"This isn't going to be enough." Jack looked at Nick.

"No, it isn't." Nick agreed, but he did not like defeat. "But we have to try … right?" Then he looked at Ilea. "Can you … I don't know … make them a doorway?"

Ilea stepped back. She nodded and moved away from the group then sat down with crisscrossed legs. Her body fell into that familiar position it had held those days and days spent healing Andy in the hospital. She reached out with her lifesong, past the stone-blocked doorway, to the people trapped in the cave. One, a young woman, was very weak, but the others were safe. Their desperate voices raged against the mountain.

Syman

Ilea wove her lifesong into the injured woman, strengthening her heart. Her body was losing blood, so Ilea helped the wounds close. Her lifesong stitched and sewed the pieces together. She could feel the woman relax as the blood slowed. This would keep her safe until the rock could be moved.

Then Ilea pulled her lifesong away from the bleeding woman and focused it on the blocked door, sweeping in and out and between the rocks that blocked the path out of the cave ... the moaning, groaning rocks. She could feel the weight of the rocks and the spaces between. She felt the massive boulders in the center of the pile and the crumbling pieces of rock that sifted in the open spaces. She could feel the wounds where the men had forced their hooks deep into the rocks.

Syman was yelling again. The people backed away to watch as his body shimmed and erupted to re-form in what looked like a bear. She had seen one of those on Nick's phone when they stayed in the lab with Vincent and Bill and Howard. Zaldi helped two men fasten a harness around Syman's new body. Then, they began to pull. Syman strained against the harness while the others pulled on the ropes with their bare hands. A man with four arms and a man with green skin. Giants and women and creatures who had no names. They all worked together.

Syman

The ropes stretched and frayed, and Ilea knew they would not ever move those rocks. So she merged her lifesong with the stone just like the shackles in the prison with Dodgen. She focused her lifesong to search for the imperfections. The weak spots in the stone that could be destroyed. Her lifesong pulled and coaxed and dissolved the frail substances that held the stone together. Bit by bit, the stones began to crumble.

Syman fought against the ropes, growling and snarling. The bear-man stumbled forward. As his right shoulder struck the ground, Syman's body flew apart. The harness hung in midair, waiting, as the pieces came back together to form the creature Jack had called a dragon. His wings jutted out the armholes in the harness, flailing, popping against the air. He drove his body forward and up.

Nick watched Ilea sitting silently behind the others, unaffected by Syman's transformation. Then he looked down at the beads around his wrist and remembered the doorway that had carried them to this world. He walked past the ropes and the chaos to sit beside his friend. She could feel his warmth as he laid his hand on her arm just above her bracelet, and just as they had in the cave, the beads began to glow. Ilea shuttered as her lifesong surged forward to fill the rocks and the cave and the people inside. Now she could both save and destroy. Her light strengthened the stone above the cave. Weaving and stitching them together so that there would be no more cave-ins, no more injuries. The woman on the ground felt the warmth of healing as her injuries faded.

Ilea could feel the hooks moving and shifting with Syman's force, so once again she drove her lifesong deeper into the rocks. Her light intertwined with the tiny pieces that meshed together to make the stone strong. Then she ripped them apart. The main stone shattered throwing the dragon against the mountainside. The men holding the ropes fell to the ground as Syman's body dropped.

For a moment no one moved or breathed. Then one by one, they stood, shaking each other's hands, slapping each other on the back, congratulating themselves in multiple languages. Jack, however, knew the truth. He looked over at Ilea, peaceful and silent, sitting beside Nick. He thought of the cave and the light and the doorway that had brought them here. He knew they were the reason the Janari was open.

The stones remaining in the doorway began to sift away like powder. The air catching the dust to carry it away. The once fearful stones now became only sand. The rocks that blocked the doorway sifted to the ground to become nothing but a dune.

Syman

Ilea drew a heavy breath then leaned over to lay her head on Nick's shoulder. "Thank you," she said in her native Tal, but he knew what she meant.

One by one, the people from inside the Janari began to climb over the sand dune, yelling at the others to come and help. Ilea felt the lifesong of the woman she had healed as she passed over the sand and out into the open air. This woman would not remember or understand what Ilea had done.

The dragon stood and shook and changed again into the ground dweller Syman. He slipped from the harness and ropes and hooks, then walked over to Nick and Ilea. His head tilted sideways as his expression grew blank. Nick had seen this behavior over and over when Syman was confronted with some new information. Something that did not make sense with what he already knew.

In a moment, Syman lifted his head and muttered, "Later. I will decipher this later." Then he walked away to continue helping with the rescue.

Departure

The next evening, they stood outside Syman's house preparing to leave. Ilea's wings quivered with excitement. Nick and Jack wore new tunics and soft pants that fit. A gift from a kind woman with four arms. Ilea tried not to look at the jagged cracks that zigzagged across the open platform and made her worry for those they would leave behind. *How will they survive without Syman?*

Syman opened his arms wide and then exploded into pieces. Tiny flecks of light hovered for an instant in the air then came back together in the shape of a saktar.

Nick shook his head. "That is the shaggiest horse I have ever seen."

Ilea did not have the words to explain that the hair on the saktar was not like the hair on his head. It was hollow in places and interlaced with bits of crystal that reflected the light and sent drops of water through the hollow spots. She grabbed Nick's hand and brought it close to the saktar. Holding his hand beneath hers, she wove their fingers beneath the saktar's hair until he could feel the coolness of its skin and coat.

Nick nodded. "That makes sense. It has a cooling system. Zaldi too?"

The saktar nodded.

"Whoa!" Jack laughed.

Nick huffed at Jack. "He can't speak, but he's still Syman. I get it."

Ilea heard the thudding steps of Zaldi as he rode in to join the group. Luna and the one-eyed Oberon rode on his back. Luna shimmered a turquoise-green as she waved to the group. Nick fought the urge to run his fingers through this almost-centaur's hair to test his cooling system theory.

"I hope Luna brought some bread," Jack mumbled, but not loud enough for anyone to hear.

Zaldi stopped beside Syman, shifting his weight from leg to leg as Oberon pulled himself over to the saktar's back. Ilea watched Oberon's every move. He would not be allowed to hurt anyone. Not while she still breathed.

Zaldi knelt so that Luna could slide from his back. She turned to remove four bags connected by long straps wrapped around Zaldi's neck then laid them across Syman's flanks.

Jack felt like he was in a bad western movie. "Saddlebags … hmmmmm."

From inside the bags, Luna took out several cloth-wrapped packages then handed then out to the travelers. Jack unwrapped his, muttering something about soap. Luna ignored his comment. Instead, she unwrapped his gift, took out the waxy bar, and rubbed it on his cheeks and nose.

Jack touched his cheeks. The scent of fruit and oil burned his eyes. "Sunscreen," he laughed. "Probably with superpowers."

But Luna didn't stop there. She brought out wide scarves and showed them how to wrap their heads and faces. Stretching up on her tiptoes, Luna put a scarf on Jack's head. Her fingers wove and patted and tucked longer than was needed to adjust a scarf.

Jack grinned, "I hope you brought some bread too."

Luna didn't understand, but she smiled anyway. Her eyes sparkled as deep as emeralds.

Syman shifted his weight and then leaned forward forcing Oberon to the ground. His body burst just as before. Pieces of light firing out in all directions, then converging in the center as Syman. The strapped bags dropped to the ground. He walked back into his home and returned carrying small packs with drawstring closures and two small skins for water. He handed one to each traveler.

"Wait a minute," Nick shook one of the water skins. "We will need way more water than this."

Syman shook his head in disagreement. "I have taken crystals from the Janari to make water. We will replenish our water each new sun. Luna has what we need."

Nick rubbed the brim of his nose and pushed his glasses back into place. "I hope you know what you're doing. I don't really want to come all this way to die our first day in the desert."

"No die," Ilea smiled. She had seen the crystals make a magic gateway, making water should be easy.

"So, Luna is coming with us?" Jack smiled at her emerald eyes.

"Yes," Syman pointed beyond the boys. "And so are they."

All eyes turned to see twenty or more people carrying bags and wearing hats and scarves for the journey. Ground dwellers stepping over the uneven places in the ground to follow two men made of gold.

"Benjee," Ilea said, noting the strange expression on Nick's face. She wanted to say that these were people her father had warned her about. People who made war. People who could not be trusted.

Jack stared at the golden-skinned men wondering if they were made of real gold. One of the men shrugged his shoulders and the gold rippled across his skin, folding under to reveal shiny, armored plates across his arms and face. Minute scales of a dragon protecting this man from the sun and wind. They each carried water skins on a strap across their chest and a long lance-like walking stick.

Nick heard the whoosh of Syman changing back into a Saktar.

Jack pounded on his own chest and pronounced his name, "Jaaaack. I am Jaaaaack."

The golden man smirked then popped his hand against his chest. "Kilp." Then he pointed to the golden man next to him. "Rilo."

Syman shook his saktar head and body making his fur stand out. Oberon had returned to his place on Syman's back along with the bags. The two of them now started for the ramped entryway into the city.

We are leaving now. Ilea shook her wings. *I will fly ahead and look for danger ... just like my brother ... just like*

Syman

Dodgen ... I will protect them from strangers ... and Oberon.
Dodgen would be proud of me just like I am proud of him.

Syman led the way out of the city and into the shadowy desert. Each of them hopeful that the ground would not shake again. Luna and Zaldi followed close to Syman. Luna had stripped down from her tunic to a thin top and shorts to expose her skin and her light. She rode as a beacon at the front of the migrating tribe — lost souls searching for their homes.

Awakening

King Kaleus awoke from his sleep, just as he always did. He stood and stretched and ran his fingers through his greasy hair. Auburn, thick and long. *How did my hair grow so fast?* He crossed the room to a small table with a stone basin and water-filled pitcher. He poured the tepid water into the bowl and splashed some on his face then dragged his wet hands through his hair to slick it back. *I need to cut it off.* He rubbed his fingers across his chin feeling the ragged unkept fur of a beard. His hands felt dirty and his nails jagged in places. He stretched again but the stiffness in his back and legs did not go away.

He crossed to the heavy-doored cabinet on the side wall that held tunics and soft pants. Clothes scattered the floor between the bed and the wall. Inside the cabinet, most of his clothes were crumpled and shoved to the back.

"Someone will pay for this," he growled, deciding on a velvety robe that hung inside the cabinet door.

Syman

Once dressed, Kaleus walked out of his room toward the great hall, just as he always did in the morning. But today, the hallway felt different, as if he was seeing it for the first time. Like a place he had not visited since he was a child. The walls looked darker and the stone floor felt cold beneath his feet. Cinching his robe tighter, he walked on until the hallway led into the great hall with a sky painted ceiling and rows of white pillars to hold it up. He stopped and studied the sky and the clouds that floated across the ceiling until he grew dizzy. *The clouds have moved. Why do the clouds look different?*

"Huh," Nela gasped. "Why are you here, my lord?" She carried his morning breakfast tray.

Kaleus stared as if she was a stranger. "Why should I not ... be here?" he snarled.

"You always take breakfast in your chambers, my lord." Nela trembled, her straight black hair falling across her eyes. Kaleus was twice her size.

"Always?" Kaleus shook his head. "When did I ever take breakfast in my chambers? I eat in the room ... the room for eating ... at my table." He put his hand to his temple and squinted his eyes. "The room with the open doors ... and the garden." *Why was it so hard to remember?*

"Yes, my lord," Nela bowed still balancing the tray. "It is just that since…" She held her tongue and waited for his anger.

"Since what?" Kaleus glared and fought the urge to grab the tiny woman and shake her until she could no longer speak.

"Since Oberon came," she said, "you have eaten in your chambers."

Kaleus clenched his fists. "Who in the red moon is Oberon?"

When she didn't answer, he could fight the anger no more. Kaleus grabbed Nela by the shoulders digging his fingers into her flesh, then shook her hard, scattering the tray and the food across the stone floor of the great hall. He lifted her tiny body from the stone floor, his arms quaking with his madness.

Kaleus looked down at the mess, then stepped backward, dropping the girl and looking up at the painted sky. His shoulders relaxed, and he sighed, heavy and low. "The last thing I remember is being gutted by one of Merith's men. I should be dead." He looked down at the whimpering girl. "But you don't seem the least bit surprised to see me alive."

Nela's hands shook. "That was a long time ago. One ... no two turns of the red moon ... maybe more ... I can't remember."

"I will have my breakfast in the hall ... with the open doors. I will eat at my table and you will stand beside me and answer every question I ask of you. You will tell me about Oberon."

Nela nodded, barely moving her head. Kaleus walked past her, stepping in the yellow nectar that pooled around the cracked tray at Nela's feet. His robe swirled across the grease and bread leaving a sticky trail and footprints on the stone floor. Nela did not turn to watch him leave.

It was hard to breath. Kaleus's anger gripped his chest, but he was also afraid. He couldn't remember the last time he had truly been afraid. That emotion had been beaten out of him long ago. But this ... this lost time ...these lost memories were terrifying. *Who was this Oberon?*

The hallway, the stone, the walls, he was remembering more of this place. He knew the way to his table. Out of this room with the tall painted sky, down the hallway past closed doors to rooms he couldn't remember. *At the end of the hallway ... that's where it will be.* Through the double-arched doors, heavy wooden doors, Kaleus walked, passing wide-eyed servants not expecting him. They scattered like leaves in a storm. He crossed the room, weaving between empty wooden tables to the front of the room, to his table, just in front of the open doors to the kitchen. To his left, three sets of glass doors to the garden were open and he could see the paved courtyard and the flowers beyond.

He took his place at the head of the table then pounded his fists against the wood. "Bring me my breakfast!" he shouted, sending the few servants still in the room rushing into the kitchen.

Nela scurried into the dining hall to stand beside Kaleus. "Forgive me my lord. Your breakfast is scattered in the main hall. I will get you something else."

"No!" Kaleus snapped. "Someone else can do that. You will stand … sit … there." He pointed to a chair at the table close to his own.

Nela stared at the chair as if it would burst into flames. She had never been asked to sit at Kaleus's table. She stepped backwards toward the kitchen and called out to several of the servants. Young girls appeared from the kitchen and Nela whispered about urgency and anger and what they should bring for Kaleus's breakfast.

Syman

"Sit down," Kaleus growled. "You are going to tell me about that Bartok Oberon and what he has done to me."

Nela pulled back a chair and silently took her place at the table. Her blue eyes round and wide and staring at Kaleus as if he were a stranger. "Oberon is your friend."

"My friends are all dead." For a moment his eyes grew misty as he faded back into Oberon's spell. Then he shook his head hard, slamming his fist against his forehead. "Dead … all my friends are dead. Merith saw to that. Whoooo is this Oberon?"

"He saved you," Nela offered. "Oberon came with blue magic and saved you."

"Blue magic," mumbled Kaleus. "I have no memory of this … Oberon or his magic."

"He has spent days and days with you."

"And what has he done? What did he do while he was here?"

Nela thought hard about all that had transpired since Oberon's arrival. "He sat with you … ate with you… met with your men in council. He was your second in command."

Syman

Kaleus slammed down both fists and stood at the end of the table. "I have no second in command. *I* am in command. He bewitched me with his blue magic … controlling me." He closed his eyes at the thought of what he might have done while under this spell. The king sighed and opened his eyes to stare at Nela. "What happened here?"

Nela tried to find a place to start. "He searched," she muttered. "He used the soldiers to search for his son … and for her … the dark-eyed one. He searched for Merith's daughter."

Kaleus pushed back his chair and began pacing the stone floor behind it, back and forth remembering the stories … the stories of Merith's daughter and how she was the dark-eyed one to fulfill the prophecy. Jaika …that was her name. He thought of the soldiers he had sent to Palon. Time and time again, small bands of men to wreak havoc in the city. Invisible soldiers who appeared from nowhere and struck without warning. Men who had killed Merith's queen and hunted his daughter.

Kaleus froze at the memories. "Did he find her?"

Nela chose her words carefully. "Yes, my lord … and others."

Syman

"Others?" Kaleus glared at Nela in confusion. "What do you mean, others?"

"He found several young girls he thought might be the dark-eyed one. It was hard to be sure. It had been so long ... she was different."

"How did he ..." Kaleus rubbed his forehead. "How did he know it was her?"

"I do not know, my lord. He did not share such things with me?" Nela didn't know much about Oberon, but she wished he was back. She had not been beaten while he was here. She had not been so afraid.

"So where is she now? The baby ... Merith's baby." Kaleus tried to remember.

He had sent soldiers ... that night ... the night Merith's daughter disappeared ... he had sent men to the castle to take the child. It had been a bluff. There were not enough soldiers to fight. The plan was to scare him ... to make Merith run with the child.

"We thought he would take her and run ... his precious Jaika ... run to the city of the Benjee or maybe even farther than that." Kaleus wrung his hands trying to force the memories to the surface. "Then we would catch them. It was a trick but ... they didn't come. We killed Benjee ... but not Merith ... what happened? I can't ..."

Without pity, Nela watched Kaleus struggle. *Maybe he won't remember. Maybe he will be changed like he was with Oberon.*

"My memories … he has taken them from me." Kaleus rubbed the back of his neck and began to pace again. "So where is she now? And where is Oberon?"

Nela was afraid to speak the truth. She lowered her head and tried to find the words. "Jaika left … on a mission for Oberon. It has been many suns. Then Oberon left … with many of the soldiers. He has not returned." She wanted to say most of the men had fled … that only a handful of soldiers had returned to the palace, but he would learn the truth soon enough.

A pale servant girl came from the kitchen to set down a cloth-covered tray of food on the table. Kaleus walked to the table and lifted the cloth. The plate was full of ganda fruit and bread. He lifted the metal plate and hurled it toward the kitchen. "When have I ever eaten ganda fruit? I have a castle full of Bartoks!"

Nela rose from her seat. "I will have them bring something else."

"Sit down!" he growled. "My head …" Kaleus dug his fingers into his hair as if he would tear it all out. "Bring me some ale!" he screamed toward the kitchen. "One of you Bartoks can surely find the ale."

Syman

The same pale servant girl as before scurried out of the kitchen with a sloshing mug of ale. She handed it to Kaleus, bowed, and ran from the room. Kaleus brought the mug to his lips and gulped down the amber liquid, emptying its contents without taking a single breath. He lowered the mug and studied the empty bottom. "Oberon has done something to me … taken my soldiers." He looked up at Nela with the wide eyes of a mad man. "Have any of the soldiers returned?"

"I do not know," Nela lied, trying again to leave from the table. "I will go and find out."

"Bring them … bring them all to me." Kaleus called after her, watching her scurry from the room, no longer believing she had the answers he sought. *Oberon needs to die,* he thought. *Merith is a part of this … I know it … he is behind this. How I hate that man.* He walked over to the double doors that led to the garden and dropped his mug on the stone walkway. He watched it clatter across the stones. Then he roared, screaming and growling to the sky, shaking his fists and dropping to his knees.

"I will have answers," he mumbled as he rose and staggered back to the table. "More ale," he groaned then slammed his fist against the table. "More ale!"

Nela could hear him shouting as she made her way to the front door of the palace. Once there, she spoke with the two young soldiers who guarded the entrance. She explained Kaleus's request and the men left to search for the few soldiers who had returned. Nela wasn't sure what to do next. She just wanted to hide. She wandered the hallways, staying in the shadows, remembering all that had taken place while Oberon was here. The suns and suns he had forced the soldiers to search for Davin. Soldiers unaware he was Oberon's only child. Davin, who could be as cruel as Kaleus when no one was looking. The hours Oberon had spent with that blue stone … with the SolStone … attempting to bring Jaika back from the other world. And the mistakes … the girls he had killed when they proved to be less than what he searched for … the girls who were not Jaika … the girls who did not bear the birthmark. This was another lie she had told Kaleus. She did know how Oberon had determined Jaika's identity. A birthmark that meant nothing to her … a tiny bird … a Picari … that's what Oberon had called it. A distinctive birthmark on Jaika's neck … a Picari.

Nela remembered preparing clean clothes and food for Jaika while she was being trained. And Seela … the kind Tal woman locked in the lower levels. The woman who had worked with the girls Oberon brought to her. The woman who could speak all languages. The woman Kaleus would remember nothing about … at least not yet. *If he could not remember Oberon, why should he remember Seela? Maybe there was time for one more lie.* Most of the guards were gone and Kaleus was lost in confusion, so this might be her only chance.

Nela went back to her room and collected a flask used to store water and some dry bread. After stopping by one of the storage rooms to collect a cloak from a hook on the wall and a small pouch, she walked down the narrow stone passageways and stairwells that led to the lower levels. The deepest level held prisoners in cold stone rooms of sunless exile, but in the midlevel, between prisoner and freedom, Kaleus ... and Oberon ... held those of special value. Here the rooms had natural light and even some amenities like pallets and blankets for sleeping. They were still prisoners on this level, but prisoners whose lives mattered. Seela was held on this level.

Nela hung the cloak around her shoulders and pulled one of her many keys from her pocket. *Seela will trust me*, she thought. *We speak each morning when I bring her food.* There were stories about the Tal and their claws, ripping people apart. Nela shuddered at the images that filled her mind. Blood ... screams ... lifeless bodies. Seela wouldn't do that ... Seela would listen ... *she will trust me*.

Oberon had promised this woman an alliance but had given her shackles instead. He had used her skills to further his own interests. Her ability to speak all languages had served him well, but he had never

119

brought her daughter, Ilea, back through the watery light. He had never kept his promise. Nela and the guard, Torin, had become her only friends. Now, Torin had fled as well. There would be no guard at Seela's door.

One, two, three, Nela counted the doors as she passed. Her hands trembled as she used her key to open the fourth door. It swung wide and Seela sat up on the small pallet she used for sleeping. Her wings sprawled across the bed and onto the floor. Nela remembered Seela's first day in this room. Her skin had been a brighter blue. Her limbs thicker, more muscled, and her long white hair had shone like the sun. It had been so long since this Tal woman had flown, Nela prayed she remembered how.

"What is happening?" Seela could see the tension in Nela's face.

Nela put her finger to her lips to quiet the questions. Then she took another key from her pocket, knelt beside the pallet bed, and unlocked the metal ankle cuff that chained Seela to the wall. Seela rubbed the dark, bloody ring of bruises that circled her left ankle. Tiny drops of blood stained the tan cloth that covered the thin mattress. Seela stood, folding her wings against her body, understanding that Nela was taking her somewhere. Usually Torin, the guard, escorted her, but today … today something else was happening.

Nela draped the cloak around the Tal woman's shoulders and pulled the hood up over her head and face. "I do not understand all that is happening," Nela whispered to the cloaked figure, "but Oberon is gone and Kaleus has no memory that you are here."

Seela turned to Nela, slipping off the hood. Her blue eyes wide with hope.

"You are leaving this place," Nela continued. "You are going to find your family. Now cover your face and follow me."

Seela quieted her fears and her joy that she would soon see her son Dodgen … her stomach twisted with thoughts of her missing daughter, Ilea. With Oberon gone, there was no hope of finding her. And her husband … Adolphus … maybe he was dead after all. She growled a little and chastised herself for losing control. She had to focus. This could be a trick. Nela served Oberon, even if he was gone. She must be ready for anything. Seela pulled the hood over her face and followed Nela out of her prison cell.

Nela led her to the end of the corridor and the stairs and upper-level door that opened into the hallway … the hallway that led to the great hall … the hallway that led to the dining room … the hallway that might lead directly to Kaleus. Nela grumbled something about being stupid and impulsive and not waiting until it was dark.

As Nela opened the door at the top of the stairway, she peered out into the empty hallway. Voices whispered frantically … somewhere … in another room. Nela could hear three or four soldiers grumbling in the great hall. Stomping about in their heavy boots and complaining about the situation. *Kaleus must not be in there. They would never speak like that in front of him.*

Nela motioned for Seela to follow. Then side by side they walked toward the double-arched doors that would open into the dining room. They walked down the empty hallway that felt as vast and endless as the sand. If they could just make it inside the dining hall, Seela would be free.

Seela pulled the cloak tighter around her body, thankful it was so large it dragged the floor, hiding her blue feet. Without warning, the doors burst open. The double-arched doors of the dining hall. Kaleus exploded into the hall barking orders and yelling about missing ale. Nela and Seela froze. Seela lowered her head in artificial reverence, wanting to conceal her face from Kaleus and doing her best to look unimportant.

"Where are my soldiers?" Kaleus snarled. He grabbed Nela by the shoulders and lifted her from the ground. "Where are they?"

Nela quivered and pointed to the great hall. The words stuck in her throat as she stared into Kaleus's glaring eyes. Burning eyes that bore into her flesh. Then he dropped her to the ground and walked away to find his men. Nela did not move until the echoes of his footsteps vanished.

Seela reached down to touch Nela's shoulder. "Come with me," she whispered. "Fly with me."

But Nela knew this frail woman was not strong enough to carry her. She would be lucky to lift her own weight into the sky. Nela patted Seela's hand then forced herself to stand, her legs still shaking. Nela nodded, and they continued down the hallway to the dining hall.

Together, Nela and Seela walked through the double arched doors. The room was filled with long empty tables. Servants worked at the front of the room still cleaning the mess left by Kaleus's anger. Broken glass and food scattered the king's table and the ground around it. But Seela could see nothing but the far wall and its doors ... three sets of doors that opened out into the garden ... a garden dripping with sunlight.

Syman

Nela and Seela weaved their way through the empty tables and out the open doors into the sunlight. Across the hand-cut brick terrace to the pathway that meandered among the garden's flowers. Draping blue flowers that grew head-high in places so that the two women were hidden from the chaos inside the palace.

Seela slipped off her hood and drank in the sunlight. She lifted her face to the sky letting the light warm her skin. Her heart ached to be in the sky.

Nela reached up and pulled the cloak from the frail woman's shoulders. "Go and find your son." She wanted to shout the words but didn't dare. Nela had listened to the soldier's stories about the crystal mines and the prisoners set free. The few soldiers who had escaped the ravages of the Breen spoke in hushed tones about the destruction they had witnessed there at the crystal mine. Nela hoped Seela's son was one of the prisoners who had escaped.

Seela nodded and stretched her wings wide. Pain tore through every bone in her back and shoulders as she let them drop. Nela could see the pin-point holes and scars that dotted the thin flesh of her wings. Wounds left from the spiked restraints Oberon had used over and over to keep her from escaping.

Syman

Nela handed Seela the pouch that held the water and bread. She knew it was not much, but it was a beginning. At least this would give her a chance.

Seela trembled with excitement and fear. Ilea was lost and her husband probably dead. But maybe ... maybe Dodgen had made it home. That's where she would start ... home.

"Thank you," she said to Nela. This tiny girl was risking her life to set her free. A life Kaleus could take at a whim. "I will come back for you."

Nela smiled, knowing that could never happen. If she returned, the soldiers would kill her on sight. This woman would be lucky to find her family. She would be lucky to stay alive. There was no time for others.

Seela nodded and then hugged Nela, pulling her close, wishing deep in her heart that she could save this girl. Nela's eyes filled with tears as Seela released her. "Fly," she whispered. "Fly away from this horrible place."

Seela turned and ran. Three steps and her wings unfurled against the air. Pain shot through her limbs, burning through her shoulders and back. Her legs shook, and she staggered but did not stop. She fought through the pain one step at a time. Her wings lifted her above the flowers. Wobbling, weaving, she made her way toward the sun. Nela watched her growing smaller and smaller in the sky. She waited for the shouting and the weapon fire that would come if the others knew Seela had escaped, but there was only the soft breeze among the flowers.

A Plan

Inside the palace at Devant, inside the great hall, Kaleus raged at his soldiers. Pacing beneath the cloud-painted ceiling, he shook his fists and roared at the 32 men still in his service.

"This is Merith's doing!?" Kaleus growled. "He sent Oberon to destroy me ... and you did nothing!"

"So, Oberon is gone?" one of the soldiers asked from the back of the room.

Kaleus narrowed his eyes. "Who speaks?"

"I, my lord." The young soldier moved toward the front of the room to stand in front of the king.

"Do you have a name?"

"My name is Davin." A young, narrow-faced man with slicked black hair stepped into view. He glared back in defiance, standing tall just as Oberon had taught him.

"Yeees," Kaleus raised his fist and knocked the soldier into the two men behind him. The king's ring left a gash in Davin's face from below his eye to his mouth.

Davin scrambled from the floor wiping the blood from his mouth and cheek.

"Will there be a problem?" Kaleus looked about the room for arguments.

"No, sir," Davin answered as he stood and backed away.

"Merith has failed." Kaleus began again. "I want him obliterated!"

"We are all that is left," said Jos, a soldier with gray streaked hair and a set of scars that lined his left cheek and forehead. "Most of the men have fled or were killed by the Breen."

Kaleus paused and scanned the room. The men were weathered. Their eyes dull and tired. Some with bandaged hands or arms in slings. The reality of this man's statement burrowed past Kaleus's anger and into his soul. His army was in shambles.

Jos stepped closer to Kaleus. "But you know we are with you until the end."

Syman

Kaleus put his hand on Jos's shoulder. He nodded toward three of the men standing behind him. "Jos, Uric, Broc ... many of you have been with me since the beginning. Since Merith's betrayal, you have fought by my side." Kaleus gripped Jos's shoulder and shook him hard. "And now, I ask you to fight with me one last time. A final blow to end Merith and his treachery."

The men cheered and growled and shook their fists to the sky. Their dull eyes now bright with promise. A bearded man with wild hair growled and grunted.

Jos gripped the king's hand that still rested on his shoulder. "It's good to have you back."

"We will fight like the old days." Uric's eyes flashed with a plan. His face worn and wrinkled like a dried animal skin. "Our men scattered in small units so that Merith could not see us."

"We will dress as commoners ... hide in plain sight," Jos added.

"We will need weapons to mask our limited numbers ... yes ... weapons." Kaleus took his hand from Jos and began to pace once again.

"Burn guns, swords ..." Broc listed the weapons they could use.

Syman

Kaleus froze beneath the painted cloud sky of the great hall. "I want butcher boxes."

The soldiers began to mumble and point out the flaws in the King's plan.

"The supply lines are gone."

"Our supply of crystals …"

"The mines … Merith has control."

"Enough!" Jos growled at the men. "Kaleus has a plan. And I agree … weapons will make up for our missing men."

Kaleus nodded and smiled, invigorated by the evolving plan of destruction. "I need enough explosives to bring down Merith's castle. I want nothing left but a pile of stone."

"And body parts," grumbled one of the soldiers from the back of the room.

"Yes!" shouted Kaleus. "And body parts. Those who stand by him … who fight with him … will die alongside him in the blast. And if Oberon is not with him, then I will hunt him down as well."

Davin held in the gasp that clawed at his throat. *Oberon … he found me, brought me here, taught me to fight. But now he's gone. He has abandoned me again. I thought he had changed.*

Syman

"We've lost the crystal mines. We will need more crystals to make enough weapons."

Kaleus glared at his men. "What do you mean weeee lost the crystal mine?" *I will not look weak in their eyes.* "Oberon did this … not you." *I can't remember. Why can't I remember?* "He will not defeat us." *I hate this man Oberon.* "We will get more crystals. We will take them from the mine. We will kill anyone who stands in our way. If Merith's soldiers guard the mine, then we will end them."

The soldiers shouted and pounded their fists against their chests in defiance of Merith.

"You," Kaleus said pointing toward the center of the room, "and you. Go … find out how many weapons we have … how many crystals. You … go and help them. And Jos," he paused, looking for the words that would not show weakness. "I need answers."

Jos could see the pleading in his King's eyes. He would not let him be shamed. "Each of you," he shouted to the room, "find what weapons you can … butcher boxes, crystals, supplies … anything we can turn to our advantage. Go … now … and do not return empty handed!"

Kaleus walked to the steps at the end of the room that led to his throne. The sparkling steps that led to the raised platform and the throne. He climbed one, two three steps and sat on the edge of the stage. He did not feel like a king. He could not bring himself to sit on the silvery throne.

With the other men gone, Jos stood before Kaleus, alone in the great hall.

"Sit beside me, old friend." Kaleus looked at the stone floor. "Tell me what this Oberon has done."

Jos sat on the steps, choosing his words and keeping a respectful distance between them. "He used the crystals. Oberon used the crystals for the people of Devant. He made new wells and gardens. He wasted them on the lowest …" Jos hesitated. He had seen the stupor that had overtaken the king once Oberon had worked his magic to save his life. There was no way to be sure what Oberon had done without Kaleus's approval. "He took the soldiers to the mines to protect it from Merith." Jos waited for the king's anger, but it did not come. "Merith freed the workers … Merith and his daughter … and the Breen." Again, Jos waited. "Keshar … Galimar … all those loyal to Merith."

"We still have workers." Kaleus kept his focus on the stone floor. "Are there not people still living in Devant?"

"Yes … of course." Jos didn't understand.

"Mmmm … then we still have workers." The answer seemed obvious to Kaleus. "Force them … pay them … take them to the mines and get more crystals. Kill those who refuse … kill Merith's men who try to stop you."

"This will take time."

"I know, but Merith will wait. He will sit in his castle with his daughter and wait. He will be fat with the overconfidence and pride that comes with victory. He will wait for me." Kaleus did not care about anything but revenge.

Jos thought of their earlier days. The days they had fought against Merith and his blindness to those in need. Kaleus had sent small groups of men into Palon to wreak havoc in the marketplace and anywhere else the people gathered. Those days of shadow fighting had now returned. He smiled to himself at the memories and his frustration with the complacency Kaleus had found with his new palace. Once they had taken Devant, their battles had become less frequent. Merith's daughter, Jaika, had vanished and so had Kaleus's taste for blood.

"Soon it will be time for the Celebration of the New Sun." Kaleus's face hardened. "The city will be busy. No one will notice us."

Jos nodded. "That is a perfect day for fighting."

Syman

"Get me my crystals and my butcher boxes." Kaleus stood beside Jos, his eyes full of fire. "We will make them all pay."

Memories

Jaika looked out across the frothy river water. The rickety bridge was gone. The bridge from her dreams and her childhood had been carried away by the river. She pulled her cloak tight around her shoulders and imagined the water tearing away the bridge one piece at a time. The same way her life had been destroyed. Since returning to Regar, she had faced every day knowing it could be her last. The endless days in Oberon's prison, the training ... Davin and his swords and guns. Even after she remembered Richard as her childhood friend and found her father, there was no certainty that any of this was true. Any of these people could have been a fraud. There was no time for sadness or memories. These were luxuries that would make her weak, so she had closed her heart, made it hard as stone, and never let herself think about all that she had lost. But today ... today she remembered.

The tears burned her cheeks at the thought of Nick and Jack and Rosie. Those who had been her life for so long. And Mattie ... for the first time since that day, she let herself remember ... the birthday ... the day everything had changed. Mattie's cold eyes and lifeless body. She knew she would never again see the woman who raised her. There was a chance to find Nick. He was still alive somewhere with Jack and Rosie. They were safe. But Mattie was gone for always.

Jaika pulled at the strap she wore around her neck that held the blue rough-cut stone that had belonged to someone who had taken her to Earth all those years ago. A woman, Mattie had said. A woman she couldn't remember. A woman who had died in the hospital where Mattie had found her. Another person lost.

Her body ached with the memories until she collapsed to the ground shaking, sobbing, covering her pain with her cloak. She ached for her home. She ached for that tiny bedroom with the bright-colored blankets ... the white house with the lace curtains. She ached to be back on Earth. She wanted to go home.

She wept until exhaustion overtook her and then laid on the ground beside the water. Sleep rescued her from the memories for a while, but when she awoke, they still surrounded her. So Jaika tried to find the good in the bad. At least she was free. As far as she knew Oberon was dead, but Kaleus and Davin were still out there. For the moment, she was safe. And there were so many happy times to remember. The days spent at

Mattie's kitchen table studying and reading. Stories of faraway lands that Mattie loved. Places she had never seen. The holidays, the dinners they had shared with her friends. The first and only time Nick kissed her.

Then she remembered the blue stone ... Oberon's SolStone. He brought her to Regar, so there had to be a way back. She was certain he was wearing it when the Breen took him away. Maybe she could find it. Maybe ... she envisioned a rotting corpse half covered in the sand with the SolStone still around his neck. It would be an impossible task.

She stood and dusted the sand off her cloak. She couldn't ask Richard for help. *How could I tell him that I don't want to be here?* He was a good man. He would always protect her, but in her heart, she loved Nick. It would be pointless to tell him. If she never returned to Earth, then Richard would never know about her feelings for Nick. So, she decided to keep her memories hidden.

She turned and walked back into the forest along a path zigzagged with black, wide-leafed vines, beneath the red Manchura trees that could block out the sun when in full bloom. Jaika remembered the endless games of hide-and-seek. The time she had spent with Richard playing in the forest. *He is a good man*, she told herself. *Richard will take care of me. I don't need to tell him about Nick.*

Syman

Jaika sat down on the ground, hugged her knees close, and looked up at the filtered rays of the sun. She scooted deeper into the viney patch, burrowing into the shadows of the underbrush. In the shadows, she felt safe, hidden away from the world and those who could hurt her. The trees rustled above her in the soft breeze. The water churned in the distance. A twig snapped, and Jaika held her breath. *Someone is here.* Footsteps ... she could hear the crunch of fallen leaves and heavy footsteps coming closer. She dug her fingers into her shins as she listened. *They found me ... they found me. Davin? Kaleus? Could Oberon still be alive?* She gritted her teeth and tried not to make a sound. With each new footfall, Jaika squeezed her legs tighter into her chest. She waited ... and waited. The footsteps came closer then moved past only to turn back toward the vines that made her invisible. Her legs began to ache from being folded. If they would just go the other way, she could stretch them out.

The leaves crunched a stone's throw away and she knew they were getting closer. She closed her eyes and listened harder. She could hear him breathing. It was a man, she was certain. His footsteps were heavy and long between. Just one man. There ... he huffed ... he was looking for something, or someone.

The leaves crunched again. *One,* she counted in her mind. One step, then another. *Three, four, five,* and he was there, standing close enough to touch. She could hear him breathing and see the vague outline of his legs through the leaves. His back was facing her, so he was vulnerable. *Maybe he doesn't know where I am. Maybe I am safe.* But Jaika knew she couldn't take that chance.

She sprung from the vines, throwing her weight against his body. Her shoulders found their mark at the back of his knee. His arms flailed the air to find his balance, but his body flipped backward into the viney patch. Jaika was pinned beneath his legs. She grabbed the straps around his leg and pulled the knife from the scabbard he wore buckled on his outer thigh.

She shoved the handle of the knife into his side and yelled, "You're dead!"

Richard reached down to cover her mouth with one hand and grabbed the knife with the other. Jaika twisted and wriggled free.

"I could have killed you," she snapped. Her dark eyes shining.

"You still need more practice," Richard smiled. He sat up. His eyes sparkling with mischief. "I've been looking for you," he scolded. "How did you know it was me?"

"I needed some time … to think." She didn't want to explain about Mattie and Nick. "I recognized your knife. It has those funny swirls."

"It isn't safe. You need to be careful. There are soldiers who still serve Kaleus."

"You sound like my father," Jaika huffed, but knew he was right.

"I hope I sound just like him." Richard leaned back on his elbows. His eyes never leaving hers. Her eyes were circled and puffy from crying. Leaves scattered her dark curls that escaped the straps she used to tie them back.

"How did you find me?" Jaika looked down at the ground, embarrassed by her red eyes.

Richard thought about the days they had spent running, hiding, playing games in this forest. "This was your favorite place when we were young. Before you were sent away. You would hide here to wait for me to find you. We threw rocks in the river and yelled into the water's roar to see if it would echo back." He touched his shirt where it hid the scar. "I knew you remembered the accident … that day on the bridge."

He reached out for her hand, but she pulled it away. "We can go back if you like. I just needed to think. So much …" Jaika didn't want to go back. She just wanted to hide.

"I know. I understand." But he didn't. Richard wanted to understand. Jaika was home now. She should be happy. *Why isn't she happy?*

They sat in uncomfortable silence beneath the trees. Jaika wiggling her feet in the dirt.

"Tell me something about where you were … before you came back here." Richard wanted to know, to understand.

Jaika smiled. This was the first time he had asked about Earth, and there were so many good things to tell. "It was different, but still the same."

Richard leaned back against a tree finding a comfortable position. It was good to see her smile.

"Only ground dwellers live there. No one gold or blue. No one can fly. But their cities are huge with tall buildings. And cars … they have cars. You would really like their cars … and motorcycles. The roads are paved, so you can go sooooo fast."

She scooted closer to him and leaned against his chest. Looking up through the Manchura trees as she described the things she had seen. The schools, the holidays, the food, but not the people. At least not all the people. Maybe someday she would tell him about

Nick. For now, his memory would live only in her heart.

Richard waited until she had run out of things to say before trying to convince her to return to the castle. "Keshar will be missing us in training. We could skip today if you like … they won't lock us away."

Jaika shook her head. "I think it would be a nice distraction."

Richard stood, towering over her, and held out his hand. She took his hand, and he lifted her from the ground like a child. Together, they walked back through the forest and into the city. Houses made of wood and stone mixed with brightly colored tents. This was the city of her memories, but it was more crowded. The streets were crowded. The spaces between the tents were filled with baskets and more people. Some wore clothes with holes and torn places patched and patched again. Others were dressed in bright colors and cloaks.

Richard could see the worry in her face. "It's growing. People escaping Devant. Merith even let a few Benjee stay."

"Benjee?" Jaika asked.

"I know. We hate the Benjee. Not as much as the Tal, but it was a first for your father." Richard kept walking. "He has even met with their leaders to discuss peace."

"And …" Jaika didn't remember Richard hating the Benjee.

"Something about the river and who should have control."

"We should share the water," Jaika thought fighting over water was a waste of time. "So, we are at war with everyone?"

"Maybe not everyone. We would fight the Tal if they were brave enough to come down out of their mountain."

Jaika remembered being taught to fear those who were not ground dwellers. She remembered the soldiers and the weapons. Oberon and Kaleus hated Merith. Richard hated the Tal. None of it made sense. "Why?"

Richard didn't answer. *She doesn't understand*, he thought. *She hasn't been here. She hasn't seen the death and destruction that I have seen. I could never make her understand.* So, they walked in silence past the tents and houses and people.

At the edge of the city, they found the clearing behind the castle where Keshar and the soldiers were training. Jaika could hear the ring of metal against metal from sword practice. Thick, heavy battle swords and those of thin, wiry metal for more civilized fighting. Marksmen fired burn guns at square targets of packed dirt and leaves. Targets with crude drawings of heads and legs and body parts. Off to the right, three men battled with no weapons at all. Sweaty, shirtless men with limbs of stone.

Jaika pointed in their direction. "I want to practice with them."

She walked toward the soldiers who took turns throwing each other to the ground amid a half-interested audience of other soldiers. Men standing, sitting, and a few laying on top of mud targets not in use. Sweaty and covered in dirt, the two men in the middle punched and grabbed and flipped each other until one eventually bested the other. Keshar, Captain of the Guard, pinned a soldier who outweighed him at least ten stones. The man grunted beneath him, shouting that he surrendered until Keshar let him up. Then the two men stood and shook hands as if nothing had ever happened.

Keshar motioned to another soldier to join him in the ring, and the entire process began again. They locked arms and began pushing and shoving each other. The fresh soldier took advantage of Keshar's age and fatigue, bobbing and weaving to keep the older man moving, but Keshar met him with a forearm to the face, sending young man to the ground. The soldier rolled then stood to dive into Keshar's knees, sending them both to the ground.

Jaika looked up at Richard. "I need to learn how to fight like that."

"You did a good job on me in the forest." Richard rubbed the back of his head.

"Yes, but you weren't trying to kill me."

"Davin and I …"

"I know." Jaika shook her head. Those day of training under Oberon and Davin were still fresh in her memories. "I was trained to kill with a sword or a knife. Oberon wanted me to kill my father. I only needed to stay alive long enough to do that. He didn't care what happened to me afterward."

Richard didn't answer.

"So, are you going to teach me, or do I ask those guys?"

The men started shouting. Jaika and Richard looked over to see Keshar and a soldier shaking hands. Keshar had bested another man.

Richard stepped out into the makeshift arena. "Captain, Jaika wants a lesson."

Keshar raised an eyebrow and wiped the blood off his cheek. "Mmmmm ... maybe you would be better suited to teach her."

"No," Jaika argued, stepping out beside Richard. "Teach me. I need to know the best way to defend myself."

The soldiers watched from the side with great interest. No one was talking or lying down anymore.

"Give me one of those." Keshar pointed to three cloth bags beside one of the soldiers. "Toss me a blade."

The soldier opened one of the bags and complied. He took out a knife like the one Richard wore strapped to his leg then threw it at Keshar. Blade over handle it flipped until Keshar caught it. The blade hit in the palm of his hand.

Keshar took the knife and poked himself in the chest several times. "This is a practice blade. It's dull so no one gets hurt. Now turn around."

Jaika looked up at Keshar. "I want to learn to fight."

"Yeees," Keshar agreed. "But first, you need to learn how to stay alive, so turn around."

Syman

Every tactic Richard and Davin had taught her was aggressive. They taught her how to attack. Maybe Keshar was right. So, she turned her back to Keshar.

Keshar reached around her, pulling her tight against his chest. The knife in his right hand went to the side of her throat. Her body shook with the memories of the battle in the mine and Oberon with his burn gun pressed to the open wound in her neck. Keshar must have felt her trembling because he relaxed his grip.

"Listen." Keshar put his mouth to her ear, whispering his instructions. "Relax. Calm your breathing. Focus on me."

She focused on her breath … long deep breaths … once, twice, listening to his voice, feeling for his heartbeat.

Keshar released his grip around her chest, reached down for her left hand, then brought it up close to her face. "Grip my hand, just below the knife."

Jaika did as he asked, still focusing on her breath.

"When you are ready, push out with your hand and turn away from the blade. You just need a little space … just a breath of air. Push, twist, and fall to the ground."

Jaika took another deep breath, listening to Keshar's words.

"Feel the motion. Wait for me to shift … to relax … to lose my focus, then you move. Be ready to get cut. Your hand will heal, but not your neck. Protect your neck. Just push and twist and fall."

Keshar tightened his grip across her chest, waiting, breathing, then looked to his left and let his hand slip. Jaika felt the change. She pushed against his hand with all her might, twisting and collapsing to the ground in one motion.

The soldiers around the circle cheered. Keshar reached down to help her stand. "It won't be that easy … you know that."

"Yes, I know." Jaika's eyes were bright. "But it is a good beginning."

Keshar tossed the dull knife to Richard. "Practice."

Richard stepped closer to Jaika, and she turned her back toward him. Together, they repeated the motions. Richard holding the knife to her throat and Jaika pushing and twisting to escape. Each time, the movements became more a part of her muscles, of her memory.

Syman

Keshar motioned for two other soldiers to come to the center of the practice area to receive instructions. Then he led Jaika and Richard away from the hand-to-hand combat to an area where the swordsmen battled. A giant of a man swung his sword into that of another soldier. The metal clashed and echoed against the stone walls of the castle.

"Jaika is right. She needs to be better prepared." Keshar watched the men finish. "And this is the man who will teach her."

Jaika smiled. "Galimar."

Keshar slapped Richard on his back. "Don't you agree?"

Galimar dismissed his opponent then cradled his sword in his arms like a child. "What have you brought me?" His face and arms showed the burns and scars he had won though battle. He no longer tried to cover them. Instead, he wore them as a badge of honor.

"This little one needs to learn to defend herself." Keshar winked at Richard.

Jaika was pleased that Galimar would be her teacher. There was no greater warrior in her opinion. Keshar described several techniques they were to practice which meant nothing to Jaika, but Galimar understood. He nodded and assured the Captain that he would take care of everything. Galimar barked at his men to pair off and go through the basic movements of the day. Then he sent Richard to find a pair of swords.

Galimar was precise and sneaky and taught Jaika ways to deceive her enemy. The three of them spent the afternoon attacking and escaping with knives and guns and other weapons Jaika had never seen. Richard seemed to learn a few new tricks as well. It felt surprisingly good to swing a sword again, especially working with Galimar. She trusted him more than anyone. He would protect her with his life.

While they trained, Galimar was called away by a messenger. Richard continued the metered swinging of his sword, but Jaika was more interested in the conversation behind them which left her open for attack. Richard sidestepped, pushed her shoulder, and sent her to the ground, bottom first. She growled and cursed and continued to watch the messenger. A frantic young soldier who spoke about escape and danger and the need for immediate action. Galimar nodded solemnly, asking questions, and eventually agreeing to help. When he rejoined them in the training circle, Jaika knew their time was over.

"There's been another escape." Galimar explained the situation to Richard as though this was an everyday occurrence. "One of them got out again."

"I see." Richard did not seem concerned. "Who do you want to lead the hunt?"

"A hunt ... what do you mean a hunt?" Jaika asked. Images of dogs chasing a fox and a hunter with a long rifle filled her thoughts. Of course, none of these things could ever happen in Palon.

"A criminal has escaped the prison," Richard continued. "We must find him. That is all."

Jaika tried to remember where the prison was and what it looked like. "Should I be afraid?"

"Of course not. I will protect you." Richard thumped his fist against his chest. "It's just one of *them*, anyway."

"Them?"

"You know. Those not from Palon. Those who look …"

"Different?" Jaika finished his sentence.

Galimar sighed. "You can do it, Richard. Take four men from the other group and see what you can find out. He'll show his head soon enough. But," his eyes narrowed, "bring him back unharmed."

"Whooo iiiiiis theeeemmm?" Jaika stood and stomped her foot.

Richard smirked at Jaika. "You know … them. Those not from Palon."

"How do you know if someone is not from Palon?" Jaika was getting irritated. The messenger was excited, even terrified, but Richard and Galimar only seemed annoyed.

"Them." Richard did not grasp her confusion. "They just look different."

"So just because they look different, they're bad?" Jaika thought about her friends on Earth. Especially Mattie. She had never seen anyone here like Mattie. Her dark skin would have made her different. Somehow the thought of soldiers chasing her Mattie, her mother … made her furious.

"Not always bad," Richard tried to explain. "But just to be safe."

"Just to be safe?" Jaika's voice rose.

"Go on." Galimar motioned to Richard. "I'll take care of Jaika."

Richard nodded and left them to join three other men with a net and ropes.

Galimar tried to explain that she shouldn't worry about such things and how her father and the soldiers took care of any dangerous people. But Jaika could not shake the image of Mattie running away from these same soldiers. Galimar grew tired of explaining and sent her back into the castle. She would have argued more, but she didn't have the energy. She dragged her feet up the steps into the castle and down the hallway toward the main hall. Maybe her father would have some answers.

Jaika peered from behind the open door of her father's work room ... his off-limits room behind the main hall. She had questioned three guards, two servants, and a cook before finding her father. And here he was ... hidden from the rest of the world, meeting with several very important looking men in long robes, squinting his eyes in analysis, solving problems that she knew nothing about. His hair, streaked with more gray than in her dreams, was still just as tousled. She heard the words Kaleus and war before they noticed her.

"I see you, little one," he smiled. Merith dismissed the others and called her inside. "Do you bring me problems or solutions, my dear?"

Jaika tiptoed inside to be greeted by what Mattie would have called a bear hug.

"Forgive me, daughter," Merith whispered his command as he released her.

Jaika's eyes brightened as she settled into one of the plush chairs beside his work table. "For what, Father?" Her feet swung back and forth without touching the ground.

"For not spending more time with you since your return. The mines ... the battles ... there has been much to do."

"I understand." But she didn't. She looked down at her swinging feet and fought the words. The words to say that she felt like an outsider since her arrival and that this place did not feel like home. Regar felt like a place from a long-forgotten dream. But it was not a dream. These people were real ... the man who had stood on the banks of the river in her dreams. The boy with a scar on his chest. A castle that sparkled with the sunlight. They were all real.

Merith's eyes softened. "I missed you ... you know? Letting you go was the hardest thing I ever did. Sometimes I wonder if it was the right thing to do."

At times Jaika had considered what life would have been like if she had not gone to Earth. She would never have known Mattie or Nick or Jack or Rosie. She couldn't imagine her life without ever knowing them.

"Something happened today," she said, "while we were training. There was an escape. Richard called it a hunt."

"Go on," Merith prodded.

"What were they hunting?" she asked, "and who escaped?" She did not understand enough about the situation to even frame her question.

Merith looked confused. "You know we have prisoners here. A few below the castle and some at the outer rim of the city."

Jaika tried to remember seeing the prisons or any prisoners.

"So, a prisoner escaped?" Jaika paused to try and understand. "What did he do wrong? Did he kill someone or steal?"

"Jaika, you can't expect me to remember the details of every prisoner we have."

Jaika wasn't sure if he was avoiding the question or truly did not remember. "So, what about most of the prisoners. Why are they there? Richard said it was because they did not look like us."

Merith squinted his eyes just as he had done with the men in long robes, assessing their abilities, their trustworthiness.

A soft knock on the door broke the spell and a soldier announced the need for the king's presence elsewhere. She watched her father leave without answering any of her questions. Jaika sat there for a long time wondering if anyone would tell her the truth.

Jaika stared at the floor as she walked down the hallway toward her room. *My father is a good man. The prisoners are dangerous. That's why he locks them away. He would not put them in the prison unless they were dangerous. He is protecting us ... so why do I feel so awful?*

The top of her head made a thud sound when she ran into Galimar's stomach. She stumbled backward then looked up into his scarred face. He was still wearing the dirt-stained clothes he had worn on the practice field. He smelled of sweat and burn rounds. The same way he had smelled that day at the mine when he had lifted her above the world. *Surely, this is a man who will tell me the truth.*

"I thought you might go looking for answers." Galimar's heavy voice echoed in the empty hallway.

Jaika was amazed at how well he knew her even though she had spent most her life in another world.

Galimar's shoulders rose and fell with a heavy sigh. "Come with me," he ordered, then turned and walked away, not waiting for her answer.

His boots thumped against the stone floor as he led the way through the castle. Jaika followed his shadow down the many hallways to one of the stairwells that led into the lower parts of the castle. The last step ended in what Jaika would have called on Earth, a wine cellar. An open space meant only for storage. Massive stone columns supported the floors above them. Columns so large that she could not have put her arms around them ... even if she had wanted to. Here and there a wooden beam angled across the top of the room or slanted in diagonal from the floor to the ceiling. The walls were lined with shelves of baskets and boxes and jugs of ale. Glass bottles filled with assorted colors that made Jaika wonder if they were food or drink or medicine ... or even poison. Large trunks with metal locks stacked four high against the only empty wall.

"Those are the crystals," Galimar explained as they passed the locked boxes, "for cooking and lights and warmth when we need it."

Jaika nodded. There could have been a dead body in there and she wouldn't have known.

Galimar led her to another set of stairs that dropped below the castle one more level. He picked up a stick that resembled a magic wand carried by wizards in one of Mattie's fairy tales. He tapped it against the stone wall, and light burst from the larger end.

"One of Richard's inventions." Galimar winked at Jaika.

They walked along a shadow-filled hallway until Jaika could see two more of Richard's magic wands hanging from the ceiling's edge. Beneath the light, two soldiers sat at a table playing a game with smooth stones and round pieces of wood.

They must have chess and checkers in every world. Jaika laughed to herself. Galimar glanced back at her giggle then introduced her to the two men playing the game. They stood the minute Galimar spoke and stiffened in attention

"We want to see the prisoners." Galimar had not asked a question.

The two men nodded and stood back against the wall to allow Galimar and Jaika to pass.

The hallway smelled of dust and grease and stale air. But it did not smell the way a prison should smell, at least not one this far beneath the castle. Jaika thought about the prison where Torin had guarded her. The cold floor and the musty air. The only light in that room had come through the door's tiny cut-out window. This place did not smell of bugs and dirt and death.

There were ten rooms, five on each side. Each one was closed off except for a door. The top of the door was made of bars of metal just like a proper prison should have. The bottom of the door was solid. There was a slight opening between the bottom and the top of the door, much like Jaika had seen in the banks on Earth where you would slide the money through. *Maybe that was where they slid the food through to the prisoners.*

She stopped to look into the first room. There were two men inside. They had rocks and round pieces of wood and seemed to be playing the same game that the guards played. There were two beds and food with blankets on the beds. The magic wands lined the hallway so that they did not live in darkness. Jaika shook her head in confusion. This place did not make any sense. *If these men were violent and evil why were they given food and beds?*

Irritated at her lack of answers, she walked to the door of the second cell. There, behind the bars, was something she had never seen. Jaika gasped and took two steps backward. The men in the first cell had looked just like her and Richard and Galimar, but the men in this cell were very different. One man had four arms and the other was a golden-skinned Benjee. Richard had said those not from Palon were our enemies. They didn't look like enemies.

In the next cell was a woman and a young girl. Both just as clean and well-fed as the others. They had light and beds and blankets and in the corner of the room she could see the same game pieces as in the first cell. Beside them lay two story books. Throughout the castle this was the first time she had seen children's books.

"Why are they here?" Jaika said, looking up at Galimar. Her back stiffened. She wanted answers. "Why are they here?" she said it louder this time.

"Your father believes it is for our safety. He still follows the old ways." Galimar closed his eyes and took a deep breath. "He is my king. So, I honor his wishes. But *my* men watch the prisoners ... not Keshar's.

This was the first time Jaika had ever heard Galimar openly disagree with her father and Keshar. *Was it always this way, or did everything change while I was gone? Maybe everything I remember is wrong.*

"Why?" She looked up at Galimar, hoping he would say more, but he didn't. He simply reached out and patted her shoulder.

"Do you wish to see the other rooms?"

Jaika nodded then walked past him to peer into the other cells. Each cell was much like the one before. Many of the people inside did not look like her ... in Richard's words ... not from Palon. *Why does looking different make them dangerous?*

"They are here just because they are different?" Jaika questioned, looking up at Galimar and trying to stand defiant and outraged, but her heart hurt too much. She loved her father and she knew he would do anything to protect her. So it was hard to believe that he would put these people in a cell just because of what they looked like.

"A long time ago," Galimar said, as he turned to walk back to the upper levels of the castle, "before you were born. Before your father was born ... or his father. We had war. Wars fought between those who did not look the same. The Tal ... the Benjee ... the white-eye Sesti and Ohmar who no longer walk the land. It was not safe to let them into the city. They would befriend us ... then betray us. Your father believes it is still that way."

"And you?" Jaika asked. She reached up to put her hand in the middle of his back to make him stop and face her, but he just kept walking. "What do you think?"

"I think we should trust your father."

He led her back to the upper levels ... back to the main hall ... where he left her.

The hunt, she thought, *I forgot to ask about the hunt.* "What about the hunt?" she shouted as he walked away, but he did not answer.

Jaika huffed then walked back to her room, dragging her feet, watching the dust scuff beneath her boots. Once inside, she closed the door then collapsed across her bed. Her mind raced with questions and worries and anger until she could think no more. So she slept until the light faded and her body drove her to get up and find something to eat.

Jaika rubbed her eyes and thought about her afternoon of training and the prisoners Galimar watched over. She still had so many questions, but they would have to wait for another day. A few splashes of water from the basin to clean her face, then she was ready … ready to find the SolStone. She did not have the power to change what her father did, but she might find the power to go home.

She skipped eating in the dining hall, meeting instead with a kind lady in the kitchen who gave her some bread and meat to take with her. Jaika made it into a sandwich just to feel a little more like she was still on Earth. She carried a cloak from her room and slipped out one of the side doors of the castle. The guards seemed unconcerned as she passed. She crossed the clearing in the back of the castle and headed into the city to find the markets.

Her morning spent crying beside the river had given her time to come up with a plan. Each time Richard or Galimar grabbed her during training, she relived each moment of the battle fought at the crystal mine. The bloody bodies, the weary prisoners, and the

Breen. When the Breen took Oberon from the mines, he was still wearing the SolStone, and the SolStone was her way to find Nick. So, the only way to get home was to find Oberon's body.

The Breen, she reasoned, could have dropped his carcass anywhere in the sand, but someone may have stumbled across it. A traveler, a soldier, someone who didn't know what the amulet could do. It was a just a necklace. If someone picked it up, or anything else from Oberon's body, they may have sold it to one of the merchants here in Palon. It was at least worth a chance to look.

The brightest tents with tassels and music sold handmade clothing and jewelry and even baked goods. The dingier tents with spliced poles and mended tears held more interesting items. Jaika went from tent to tent, avoiding the more expensive merchandise to study the just-a-little-better-than-trash items for sale: broken knife blades, gun barrels, fragments of what might have been a crystal, strong smelling potions and oils to help with sleep or pain, or to stop an enemy.

Em, a kind old man with weathered skin, tried to help with her search. Jaika described the necklace with its bent metal edges and broken blue-glass stone in the center. She though it was a crystal, but it could easily pass for melted sand used for windows. She emphasized the damage to make it seem less valuable.

"Like a window in the middle," she said, "with a piece missing." It wasn't really a lie. She didn't know for sure what it was made of. She also left out the glowing part. "I don't think it was valuable. It belonged to a friend of my mother."

"You lost your mother?" Em asked.

"Yes … yes, she died … I was just hoping I might …"

Em's eyes sparkled with kindness. "Perhaps I could contact you if I find what you are looking for?"

Jaika knew she couldn't tell him who she was. "I will come back … another time."

"You never know. You may find what you seek." Em nodded and smiled. "There are more sellers further out from the city. Maybe you will have luck with them."

Jaika smiled at his encouragement. *Tomorrow*, she thought, *tomorrow I will go farther into the city. And the next day and the next. But for now, the others will be looking for me.*

Transport

Ilea could feel the weariness in her wings as well as those in the caravan who walked beneath her. Their feet snaked trails in the sand and their shoulders slumped. Three men toward the end of the line of travelers sat down to wait for their strength to return.

She landed in front of Syman, still a saktar, and still carrying Oberon. "We can't keep going," Ilea told him as she folded her wings behind her shoulders. "*They* can't keep going. Some have already stopped to rest."

Syman knelt on his front legs, and Oberon slid to the ground. Ilea watched him hobble and stumble away from the saktar. She knew she should offer to help him … but she didn't.

Syman shimmered and exploded into dust, then his body reformed as the Syman she recognized. Zaldi turned his upper body around to lift Luna from his back. His arms rippled with strength. Once they stopped, so did the rest of the travelers, dropping their

165

packs, and sitting down in the soft sand. Jack offered to help Luna carry the bags she was unloading from Zaldi's flanks.

"We can stop here. Begin construction of the sunblocks." Syman spoke clear and loud so that those around him could hear.

The people scattered. They opened their packs and dragged out paper-thin cloth that shimmered silver in the moonlight. Sticks no longer than a man's forearm telescoped out then clipped together at the ends to make a skeleton frame for the fabric. Syman built one for them as well with parts taken from the bags he had carried.

Nick watched in awe as the teepees quickly took shape. The silver fabric was lighter and thinner than any he had seen on Earth. So simple. The frame, the cloth, the structures went together as simple as a child's toy. *How can these people have such advanced materials? They live in caves and yet ...*

As they worked, the orange and yellow of the sun's morning light appeared above the mountains on the horizon bringing with it the wind. The approaching heat sent the travelers crawling inside their sunblockers. There they unrolled mats and prepared to sleep. Nick and Jack went inside the structure Syman had built. To their surprise, they could still see the mountains and the sand and the sun. The view was hazy, like looking through a smudged window or a wall of water, but the outside world was framed within the metal bones of the tent. The see-through walls left Jack feeling exposed and vulnerable.

"I feel like everyone is looking in." He put his hand on the fabric wall. "I guess they will get a nice view of me snoring and drooling while I sleep."

"They can't see in. The walls are silver, remember, a little like a two-way mirror." Nick tried to reassure his friend, but he also felt like they were inside a glass house. He studied the fabric rippling with the winds that came with the sun and felt the cool air that passed through. The weave of the cloth filtered out the heat. *How did they make this?*

Nick and Jack watched through the sides of the tent as Ilea and Syman walked toward them carrying woven mats. There was easily enough room for five or six people to rest comfortably, so once they were all inside, they spread out the mats and found a comfortable position. Nick stared up at the sunbaked sky listening to the flapping of the see-through cloth as he drifted off to sleep in the coolness of the sunblocker.

The sun was setting when Nick awoke to the sound of water dripping, splashing, gurgling along with mumbled words and laughter. He stretched beneath the purple-gray sky, then rolled over on his stomach. His tent was empty, and the water sounds were coming from just outside. One of the tents had been stripped of its cover. A shoe-sized box hung by straps from the intersecting framework at the top. And from that box poured the water. It fell in spurts and gushes onto a sleeping mat beneath it. People took turns filling their flasks and splashing each other in the process, walking beneath it, shaking and wiggling like puppies after a bath. Zaldi stood beside them, vigilant and calm, his arms crossed. Nick was glad he was on their side. Jack stood with Luna, her skin glowing pale yellow-green in the dying sunlight.

He stood and walked outside to join the others. Despite the rough terrain, the heat, and the endless walking that lay ahead, these people were happy. Their unfamiliar words rang with joy and peace. A hundred different species working together to survive. Nick couldn't stop the nagging doubt that this scene couldn't go on forever. People working together ... helping ... sharing. Somewhere in this place of eternal sand, there was a something or someone who could destroy it all.

The tents behind him began collapsing to the ground. Their coverings folded into piles no bigger than a man's palm. The camp was disappearing. Jack handed him a flask and some leathery food that made him think of beef jerky.

"Way better than snake bacon," Jack mused, smiling at Luna.

A shadow of wings caught his eye, and Nick watched as Ilea and another Tal man landed at the edge of the camp. The man shimmered. His pieces scattered, and again, he was Syman. They walked together to the water box.

"We know the way," Ilea announced as they came closer.

"I'll bet you do," Jack snickered and raised his eyebrows.

Syman spoke with Zaldi in their strange language. Then the almost-centaur rode through the camp, pointing and giving orders. The tents were soon packed, and the last of the travelers made their way to the water box to fill their flasks. Jack helped take apart their own tent, while Syman unstrapped the water box from the empty frame. From within the box, he removed two white crystals and a blue one, wrapped them in separate cloths, then tucked them in one of the bags he carried each day across his back.

The sky was filled with stars as the caravan continued its journey across the sand. Syman again carried Oberon while Luna rode with Zaldi. Ilea would fly, circling about the travelers, then land again to walk beside Nick and the others. They traveled together toward the red moon. Jack walked in between Syman and Zaldi. Looking up at Luna with shining eyes. But he also watched Oberon fighting to stay seated atop Syman's swaying back. As the night wore on, Jack could no longer fight his curiosity.

"So, what happened to you, anyway?" Jack spoke with Oberon as if they had known each other a long time. "Did you make somebody mad?"

Ilea giggled softly behind them.

"In a way," Oberon answered, not bothering to look at Jack. "There was a war. Many were injured or killed."

Jack shook his head. "So, who started it?"

"It started a long time ago." Oberon paused, thinking about his hatred for Merith, the battles fought between Palon and Kaleus and the other cities. "It was my fault as well."

"Why?"

Jack's question was clear and short and without room for the intricacies of the anger and jealousy and fear and greed that cause wars. "I wanted more for my son. I wanted a kingdom to take him out of poverty and give him a life of significance."

Jack nodded. "I guess I can understand that ... wanting good things for your son. So, did you kill a lot of people?"

"A few." Oberon's shoulder's slumped as he hung on to Syman's fur. "The soldiers ... I had the soldiers kill ... I ... I ..." He stumbled on the words.

"So, you are not a very nice person, are you?" Jack's words held no condemnation, only his assessment of the situation.

Oberon looked up at the stars. Everything he had done seemed logical. At least at the time. He had wanted to be more ... to have more.

"So, what did your son want?" Jack thought he probably would have liked a nice cheeseburger. "Did he want a kingdom with you?"

"I didn't ask him."

Jack shook his head. "You need to talk more with your son. That's what a good father does." *At least that's what I wish mine had done.*

Oberon felt a hollow emptiness in his back. "I never told him."

"Told him what?"

Syman

"I never told him I was his father."

Jack bit his lip and tried to think of something nice to say.

Oberon grunted. "Everything started with the stone. Galimar and Jaika and the stone." His voice rose with anger. "If I could go back, I would stop Galimar from destroying it. I would not let him send Jaika away. I would change everything."

Ilea's wings twitched. "You mean the SolStone." Ilea stopped and stared at Oberon. "The one you used to send me away. The one you keep hidden." Her claws opened and her eyes flashed with anger.

Beneath Oberon, Syman slid to a stop in the sand. And with a ripple, the others behind him stopped as well.

Oberon put his hand to his heart and glared at Ilea with his one eye. "How can you know that?"

"It sings to me … just like all the crystals do."

Syman shook all over, then vanished into a million pieces dropping Oberon and the bags in the sand with a thud. He came back together as Syman the man.

"You … have … a Sulstun?" Syman asked.

Syman

For an instant, Nick thought this robot of a man had finally found his anger, but it disappeared as quickly as it began.

"Give me the Sulstun," Syman ordered, looking down at Oberon squirming in the sand.

Oberon lifted it from beneath his shirt and around his neck. The blue light began to pulse as he handed it to Syman.

"You are Tal." Syman said, looking over at Ilea.

She glanced sideways at Nick, not sure what being Tal had to do with the stone. "Yes," she answered.

"Your parents are Tal," Syman continued.

"Yeeees," Ilea still did not understand.

"Then you can use the Sulstun. You are Tal."

Ilea twitched her wings with impatience. "I don't understand."

"Just like your bracelet. You can use the Sulstun to transport greater distances."

Ilea's eyes grew wide. "I am nothing. I cannot use the SolStone?" She spoke in the Tal language, so Nick and Jack were not sure why she was upset.

Oberon glared and tried to stand. *Why does he call it the Sulstun? Why does he think a Tal can use it? She is nothing. They are nothing. They can't even say the name of the amulet.*

Syman held out the stone to Ilea, but she backed away. "No," she repeated, "no." The stone was meant for someone more powerful than her.

Syman could see Jack working his way around Zaldi to get closer to Ilea, so he began speaking words he would understand. "I can teach you. You have the power to transport to Palon." Then he repeated the words in Tal.

"So, she could help us travel faster?" Nick knew such a crystal had brought them to this place. Maybe it could take them to Ilea's home. Maybe they wouldn't have to walk all the way across this desert.

"Yes," Syman answered. "She has the ability to transport us closer to Luz … closer to Palon."

Ilea looked at Nick. "You can do this," he encouraged. "Just like in the mine."

Ilea ruffled her wings. She looked behind her at the travelers already weary after only two nights of walking. She looked at Jack and Nick and Oberon still pushing at the sand. *If Nick believes, then so do I. After all, I have done this before, sort of.*

174

Syman

"Show me what to do," she said as she stepped closer to Syman.

Syman laid the stone in her hand. "Just like your bracelet, it will hear you."

Ilea nodded, still not truly understanding. Her bracelet knew what to do. She didn't control it.

"You may not be able to take us all the way to Palon or Luz at one time, but you can transport us across the sand in small steps. I calculate that four transports will easily put us within visual range of Palon."

Ilea listened and tried to image them moving across the sand.

Syman told her to imagine a doorway. A round opening of blue-white light that they could pass through. As Syman described the wall of light, she understood. She had already been through such a doorway. Oberon had used one to send her away, and somehow, she had used the crystals in their bracelets to bring them back through. A doorway that had carried her and Jack and Nick back to Regar.

"Yes," she nodded. She knew exactly what a transport doorway should look like.

Syman led her out into the sand, a safe distance away from the others. He lifted her hand toward her heart. The hand that held the stone. "See the light. You know what it should look like. Think of Palon and Luz. That is where you want to go. Hold the image in your mind ... see yourself walking through the light to Palon on the other side."

She closed her eyes, squeezed the stone with her fingers, and whispered, "Take me to Palon. I want to see Palon."

In front of her eyes, a blue-white light appeared. It spiraled outward causing the air to churn and boil. It grew, swallowing the darkness until the watery wall of light was large enough to walk through.

As Oberon watched, he remembered the suns and suns he had spent practicing with that stone, guiding it, forcing it to follow his command. Yet he had never truly mastered it. This blue girl had done it in one try, and he hated her for it.

Ilea began to shake and stumble backward in the sand. Her wings opened to fight the air. The light pulsed, growing brighter and brighter, then exploded outward and disappeared.

Ilea fell to the ground, trembling, shaking. Her eyes burning and blurred with the flash of light. Her strength empty.

Syman

"She needs to rest," Luna warned Syman. She had been watching from atop Zaldi. "Ride with me, and when you are stronger, you can try again."

Nick helped lift Ilea to sit in front of Luna. There, she leaned against Zaldi's torso to keep her balance. Syman put the Sulstun in his bag and, once again, the caravan began to move toward the red moon.

The Trail Home

Seela could see the cliffs of her mountain home of Luz. The last drops of the water Nela had given her were gone, and she lay in the sand with her wings spread wide gathering her strength. The city was so close, she could almost hear the people talking. Her shoulders and back felt like stone. Her wings numb. Her days working for Oberon had bled one into another until she had lost count. She had helped him find his son. She had interpreted and taught language to whomever he wished, but Ilea was still lost. Her hope and her strength had failed. The SolStone had proven to be more difficult to control than expected, or maybe Oberon was just a liar and a fraud. Either way, he had not been able to bring back her daughter. But if she could make it home, maybe Dodgen was there. Maybe he had found Ilea. Maybe …

Seela pulled her wings close and stood in the sand, her legs shaking. She forced her feet to move. One step then another. The sand sifting between her claws. Her wings dragged the ground behind her as she started to run. One, two, three steps, her wings lifted and pulsed. Her body rose above the sand, lurching, jerking, desperately fighting the air. Higher and higher her wings brought her closer to the lights in the sky. But her strength was spent. The mountains became blurred gray stone on the horizon. The lights vanished, and she fell. Heavy as stone, her wings collapsed without a fight. Her bones prepared to hit the ground.

Then, Seela heard the *vhoom* of Tal wings. She felt her body rise as a blur of heavy arms wrapped around her. Her head rested against a rock-hard shoulder, and she let herself go limp against his warmth.

"It's time to come home."

The man spoke, and Seela knew the sound. Better than the sound of her own voice. Adolphus soothed her with his words and carried her home.

#

Beneath the palace, inside one of the weapons rooms, Jos wrapped the last of the butcher boxes and placed them into the padded compartments of the bags the men would carry into Palon. They had scrounged enough parts to make 23 of the explosives. Kaleus had wanted more, but this would have to be enough.

Jos closed the final bag, and then scratched the scars on his left cheek. A knife blade and a fall from a saktar had given him those scars. He thought of his younger days, when he had ridden beside Kaleus and the twenty or so men that had joined their mob. They had fought in darkness, attacking in scattered groups to cause as much chaos as possible. Throwing fire crystals and detonating butcher boxes. They had even managed to kill Merith's queen and eventually take the palace here at Devant. Merith and his self-righteousness had given them plenty to hate.

"How many?" Uric asked as he and Davin entered the room. They were dressed as simple merchants. There would be no black uniforms today.

"Twenty-three." Jos handed Uric one of the bags. "Did Kaleus send both of you?" Jos didn't trust Davin. He had been Oberon's favorite.

Uric nodded and looked down at Davin. "He doesn't care who brings him the boxes, just as long as they're ready."

"The men have already packed supplies to make the journey to Palon." Davin tried to sound confident. Oberon had made it easy. Under his leadership, the men had no choice but to accept him ... to follow his orders. But now, with Oberon missing, the balance of power had changed, and he had a fresh scar on his face to prove it.

Jos divided the bags among them, and they carried them to the open courtyard outside the front gates. There they found Kaleus with his remaining men and more than enough saktars. As with Uric and Davin, the men were dressed in simple tunics and baggy pants, the well-worn, tattered clothes of street people.

The doors to the palace were open wide and the saktars trampled the yellow and blue flowers that grew around the courtyard. The men kicked rocks and dirt into the stone basin filled with water in the center of the pathway circling the courtyard.

Kaleus picked up a knee-high statue of a woman that stood by the open front doors and shattered it against the side of the basin. He grunted and yelled out at his men. "Whatever happens today, I am not coming back here!"

The men cheered and joined in the chaos. The servants watched from the windows and open doors as the men destroyed the courtyard. Jos pried stones from the pathway and tossed them into the water. Uric and his brother smashed the remaining statues. Three saktars bolted, trampling the tallest flowers as they ran through the garden. The men shouted and threw rocks at the escaping saktars, driving them further into the garden. Davin watched in silence.

"Enough!" growled Kaleus. "We will have our revenge!"

Again the men cheered as they climbed aboard their saktars. Jos and Uric and Davin secured the butcher boxes to their own mounts for safekeeping. The sun was low in the sky as they headed out across the sand to destroy Palon.

From the highest tower in the palace of Devant, the Krill known as Levek watched all that transpired below, his tentacles wrapping beneath him, raising him to the height of the window. He had waited patiently for this day. The day that Kaleus would leave the palace to follow another path. The day he would no longer be needed in Devant.

Levek had lived in the palace since the Makers had abandoned him. Hidden from the king, he worked only with the few who knew of his existence. He had been faithful to heal the worthy … the gentle and weak who could not protect themselves. He had protected Jaika during her time in the palace. Healing her wounds after each of Davin's training sessions, keeping her lifesong strong. He would do it again in the upcoming battle, if necessary, but he must consider all the people. Regar was facing new dangers now, and his ever weakening lifesong would be stronger if it was no longer scattered across the planet. It was time to leave.

Levek pulled his tentacles close to his body, closed his eyes, and released his lifesong. The fleshy body that had once been Levek collapsed to the ground in a mass of tentacles. The tunic he wore to hide his ever-changing shape puddled to the floor atop his lifeless body. He had no need for either of them. He would have a new body. His lifesong would now be in Luz. His lifesong would join with the one they called Adolphus.

#

Beneath the setting sun, Nick and Jack helped Syman disassemble the sunblocker they had shared with Ilea during the heat of the day. Ilea had ridden with Luna until the sunrise, then spent the light hours sleeping. Nick had forced her awake to eat and drink. The SolStone had weakened her more than Syman had expected. But it was growing dark now, and she would try again.

"I don't think she is ready," Nick argued. "She is still so weak."

Syman

Syman listened to Nick's concerns but did not change his mind. "The Tal have used the Sulstun for transport since the Makers created them. She has the proper coding. Her abilities have simply heightened her connection, so she must weaken her approach."

"So, she's trying too hard? Is that what you are saying?" Nick didn't think it was worth risking her life.

"Nobody has ever told me to try lesser." Jack grinned. "Is lesser a word?"

"No." Nick snapped. "It's not a word. Either way, she could get hurt."

"Yeah." Jack took Nick's side. "If Nick says it's too dangerous, then…"

Ilea dropped to the ground beside them, fluttering her wings closed behind her. Her time spent flying beneath the sun had revived her weakened lifesong. She stretched her neck and rolled her shoulders. Behind Nick she could see the travelers taking down their sunblockers and packing their bags. She knew she had to try and help them. "I feel strong. I am ready to make the SolStone work."

Syman removed the amulet from his neck and handed it to Ilea, then together they walked out into the sand. "You cannot use all of your strength. You cannot try to alter the lifesong of the crystal. Simply reach out, speak to it, do not force it to comply."

Ilea thought of Dodgen and the many times he had laughed at her for *torturing the stones* as he called it. As a child, she would send her lifesong into the rocks and find the crystals within. She used this skill to make her jewelry, to make the bracelet Nick wore. The bracelet she had given to Jaika. And eventually, she had been able to destroy the shackles that had held Dodgen in the prison at Devant. She had torn them apart from the inside. Today ... she would have to be careful not to do that to the SolStone.

"I think I understand what to do." Ilea held the stone in her hand. "I will be kind."

Syman considered her choice of words. Kindness did not seem to apply to the Sulstun, but not everything has to make sense. According to the Maker, *not everything has to make sense.*

"You may begin." Syman stepped back.

This time Ilea sat down in the sand and listened to the stone. She let her lifesong wash over it, finding its patterns, finding its pain along the jagged hole cut into its side and the jagged cracks through its center. Just like the people she had healed. Just like Oberon, just like Andy, the stone cried out to be healed. Softly, she began to sing. Her song of life and courage. The stone was not hers to command but to guide and heal.

In her hand, the stone began to glow. A whisper of blue-white light pulsed from the center of the stone, gently growing in strength. Again, a spiraling light appeared in the air above the sand, but this time it settled further out in front of Syman. Away from the caravan of travelers. The light was soft and grew in gentle bursts until the doorway opened to its full size. The watery light shimmered and waited.

"What is on the other side?" Syman asked, but Ilea did not answer. Her focus remained on the stone.

Syman walked to the light and then through the doorway. Ilea did not move. Within moments Syman returned. He nodded and motioned for the others to follow.

"Is the city on the other side?"

"Does this lead to Palon?"

Voices in the crowd shouted their questions to Syman.

"Yes!" He shouted in his cold, clear voice. "This is the first doorway to Palon. Follow me."

Hostage

Night after night, Jaika snuck away from the castle and into the city, traveling from tent to tent, studying the merchandise. Finding the SolStone was all she could think about. Jaika wore her hood over her face as she wandered through Palon. This city that went on forever. It twined around the ends and front of the castle surrounding it on all sides. Parts of the city had their own distinct music and food and personality. She could just as easily find herself bathed in the aroma of greasy meat or the warmth of baking bread. Women shouted at their children. Old men drank and laughed and talked about their past. She saw a lady with an eyepatch and a giant of a man with white eyes. The city was filled with happiness and grief and was nothing like the world she had known with Mattie.

Jaika was careful not to follow the same path twice. She didn't want to become a familiar face. She didn't want anyone to know she was the daughter of the king. On occasion, she would buy something if the merchant was especially kind or seemed in desperate need of funds. Sweet breads were her favorite indulgence.

Each night when she returned to the castle, no one questioned her absence. No one asked about missing dinner. Everyone was busy with their own work. So, her evening journeys grew longer and longer, and Jaika grew more fearless. Tonight, she would travel further into the city than she had ever gone. Tonight, she was going outside the wall.

The city was surrounded by a stone wall that could be fortified and locked down during an attack. A wall that served as a lookout post for a handful of soldiers. A wall that meant safety and protection. If anyone had found Oberon's body, surely the SolStone would have been sold here.

The crowds were heavier tonight. The Celebration of the New Sun had already begun, and it would be easier to hide. Jaika walked past the brightest colored tents through the heart of the market and out to the places at the edge of the city where many were afraid to go. As she walked beneath one of the archway doors in the wall, she felt the weight of its shadow across her back, as well as the two soldiers perched above the archway watching her and any others who walked beneath it. On the other side … on the outside, Merith's men could no longer protect her.

Syman

The air was cool tonight, so she pulled her cloak tight across her stomach. The others in the marketplace did the same. A sea of cloaks hid the eyes and faces she was used to watching and made her chest tighten with worry. *Maybe coming here was a mistake.*

"No," she whispered against the darkness. "I will find a way home."

In the first tent, a man, with a dark beard so long it hung outside his hood, shook her hand and welcomed her to his shop. Jaika worked her way through his tent looking over the jewelry, the scattered pieces of metal, and even the broken pieces kept in the back. Any remnant that might lead to the blue stone. Even with his face covered, she could tell he was watching. Jaika thanked him and moved on, but she couldn't shake the sensation that they had met before … somewhere outside this tent.

Being on the other side of the wall had left her jittery and uneasy. Maybe it was just her nerves or imagination, but she kept a close eye on those around her — the merchants, those who shopped, and most importantly, those who did not. *Breathe, just like Galimar said, breathe.*

Jaika continued searching the closest tents without any luck. So, she decided to take a chance on the last few tents farther out. She would check those three and then go back to the castle. As she moved closer, she could see that the last tent was not that of a merchant. Instead it held wooden tables and drunken men staggering around the doorway. From inside, she could hear the people laughing and making other questionable noises. *I will go into the first tent ... maybe just the first one.* If she turned back now, she would be forever haunted with the possibility of finding the stone if she had only kept going. So, she counted, *1, 2, 3.* In her thoughts, she counted the steps to the next tent. Jaika pushed her feet forward. *This is for Nick. The only way to find Nick ... 7, 8, 9.*

Jaika was relieved to see an old woman sitting inside the first tent. She smiled with her three teeth and welcomed Jaika inside. Her goods were scattered out on rows of blankets in the dirt, sorted by size and color and no logic whatsoever. It took her only a few moments to scour the room and understand that there was nothing here to help her find Nick. As she turned to leave, the bearded man from the first tent stood beside her. His hood was pulled down and his wild hair and beard exposed. Their eyes locked and, for a moment in her memories, she was surrounded by soldiers in the palace in Devant.

Jaika pulled her hood down around her face and looked away. She felt the bearded man walk past her, then she slowly edged toward the doorway. But as she turned to leave, there was another man blocking her path. He did not wear a hood and beneath his half-open cloak, she could see a sword strapped to his belt.

"I have something to show you," he said, watching Jaika squirm. "You *will* come with me."

He turned and walked away from the tent. Jaika froze, waiting for her chance to bolt. Before she could escape, she felt a steel hand on her shoulder and a voice against her neck. "Follow him ... princess."

Jaika felt the blood in her body rush to the ground to cement her feet to the floor. Her wooden arms and legs refused to move. Her chest tightened, so she took a deep breath, hearing Keshar and Galimar speaking in her head. *Remain calm, center yourself, watch for their mistakes.* Three painfully slow breaths then she stepped forward. The man behind her kept his hand on her shoulder. The other hand that she couldn't feel was most certainly on a weapon. She wouldn't let herself think about it.

They walked out of the tent, past two more cloaked men who all followed the bearded man until they came to a wooden table outside the last tent. The tent that held laughing men, drinking and eating and watching her. Laughing men who paid no attention to the body lying on the table. His hands and feet tied like a wild animal to be roasted. He wasn't dead. She watched his chest rise and fall. There were blood stains on the wooden table and a gash above his left eye

"He was following you." The bearded man chuckled as he turned to walk backward and stare at her hooded face. "That's how we caught him, little princess. He was watching you when he should have been watching us." He laughed again, pleased with himself.

The man on the table moaned. Jaika jerked away from the soldier behind her to rush to his side. One of the cloaked men raised his hand for the others to wait.

"Richard," she whispered, touching his forehead. She ran her fingers along his scalp to search for more injuries.

"He's alright," said a voice behind her. A voice that sent a chill across her back.

She turned to stare at the stranger as he pulled down his hood to expose his red hair and glaring eyes. His beard was clipped and precise. His face clear and focused. This was not the hazy-eyed Kaleus she had known in the palace. He no longer wore the silvery boots or elaborate capes. He was dressed just like everyone else. He could have been any common man in the city except for the hatred oozing from his skin, dripping to the ground. This man was ready to kill her.

"But he won't continue to be alright, unless …"

Jaika shuddered. She closed her eyes and breathed deeply, counting, *1, 2, 3.* There was no room for mistakes. "What do you want me to do?"

"I will explain, eventually." Kaleus smiled. "For now, I just need you to stay close. It is very simple little princess. If you escape, he dies."

Then Kaleus hesitated. This had been an unexpected bit of good fortune. To find Merith's daughter and Richard. The boy who had lived and worked in his home, pretending to serve, while being loyal to Merith. He deserved whatever happened to him. But Jaika, she could be used as leverage.

"Uric, check her for anything we can trade."

Jaika stepped away from Richard. The man who had held her by the shoulder grabbed her and pulled her hard against his body. He ran his hands across her stomach and waist, finally grabbing at a tiny bag tied to her belt.

He jerked it free then shook it in front of her face. The metal pieces jingled inside. "I'll wager there's something in here."

She grunted and bit her lip. While he was gloating and distracted she knew she could take him to his knees, but then Kaleus would kill Richard. She would have to wait ... there would be a time ... another time.

The soldier threw the bag to Kaleus and he opened it. "Yes, this will get us a place to wait." Kaleus motioned to another man who stood inside the tent, looking like just another drunk. "Jos."

The man nodded and moved out into the open. Jaika watched Kaleus slap him on the shoulder. "It's time, my friend. Go and tell the others to begin the plan. Remind them to be strategic. To find places that will cause the most damage."

Jaika's heartbeat quickened. *He's planting weapons ... He's going to destroy the city.* She watched Kaleus and Jos and the others through a fog of fear and darkness. *Galimar would know what to do,* she told herself. *What would he do?* Then a younger soldier caught her eye. A hooded soldier standing behind the table ... behind Richard. He smiled, and her chest felt hollow and dead.

"Davin," she whispered, hoping with all her heart that she was wrong. That he was not here.

"Hello, little Picari." Davin spoke from beneath the hood.

Kaleus watched Jaika grow pale at Davin's voice and he knew this young man was part of something forgotten. Something Oberon had done. Something he could use to his advantage.

Jos nodded to the bearded man, who then lifted Richard from the table, throwing him across his shoulders like a sack of grain. "Where do I take him?"

"Follow me," Kaleus smiled at Jaika. His mouth twisted and gnarled. "And … you," he ordered Davin, "stay close to her."

Jaika swallowed hard and counted. *1 … 2 … 3.*

The bearded man followed Kaleus. Uric shoved Jaika in the back and growled, "Let's get going pretty one." Davin simply nodded and smiled and walked beside her.

They walked away from the tents and through the arched gateway of the city wall. Beneath the pointless guards who watched them walk … who watched the bearded man carry a body past the wall and into the city without a single question. Jaika could have called out. She could see their faces. They would hear her scream, but it would be too late by the time they climbed to the ground. So, she counted … *17, 18, 19. Stay focused, 22, 23, 24.* They made their way into Palon.

Kaleus was careful to keep his face covered while Uric asked questions from passing strangers.

Jaika could see the men pointing and nodding as they made their way along the dirt road to a tavern with a sign hanging above the door that read *Saktar's Run*. Uric went inside and then came back with a key. Jaika kept an eye on Davin and the bearded man who still carried Richard.

They walked to the back of the tavern and up the stairs to the rooms above. Jaika thought about the time Richard and Davin had brought her to just such a place so that she could kill Merith. As Uric shoved Jaika through the door to the bedroom, she fell. Her body spun, and she pitched forward with all her strength to grab Uric around the waist. He fought to untangle himself, digging his fingers into her neck and arm. As she slid to the ground, she grabbed the handle of the knife he kept strapped to his leg and pulled it from the sheath. Jaika collapsed to the ground holding her stomach and crying out in pain. Her cloak puddled around her. This gave her a moment to lift her tunic and slide the knife inside the waist of her pants along her hip before the soldier grabbed her arm and jerked her to stand.

"Are you playing games?" he growled into her face, his breath smelling of ale and smoke. He gripped her by the shoulder and shook her hard. Half-dragging and half-lifting, he pulled her into the room. Uric shoved her against the wall. Jaika was careful to fall with the knife facing upward. She cowered against the wall pulling her cloak around her and lowering her head to prepare for a kick or fist. But the soldier turned away.

The bearded man dropped Richard onto the bed then struck him in the face. Blood ran from his mouth and nose as the soldier jerked on the ropes that held his wrists to doublecheck their strength.

Kaleus stood in front of Jaika watching her huddle against the wall.

"How long until the others return?" the bearded man asked.

"They need to find sixteen locations for the explosives," Uric said, "so, they should be back before morning."

Jaika looked over at Richard bleeding on the bed. Her heart sank. *They will destroy the city and the castle and all those inside. Then eventually Richard and me.*

Kaleus nodded to the bearded man and Uric and Davin. "Stay outside ... all of you ... watch the door and the road to this place. I need some ... alone time with the princess."

Uric sneered and laughed. "Enjoy yourself."

Jaika gasped and scooted closer to the wall. She knew what a cruel man could do to a woman. Then she remembered the knife hidden beneath her cloak and vowed that Kaleus would know her blade. She would fight him with all her strength.

Kaleus sat down on the edge of the bed beside Richard. "I saw what you did." He rubbed his beard. "Taking Uric's knife. Not bad for a princess."

Jaika swallowed hard.

"You can keep it for now," he said, then reached to the scabbard strapped across his back and pulled out a jagged-blade knife the length of her forearm. "Now this knife we're going to save for your friend Richard, here." He tapped the flat part of the knife against Richard's leg. "I am especially angry with him. Lying about who he was. Pretending to serve me. He deserves a much bigger knife. But you ... you are not going to lie to me, are you?" He wiped the knife across his pants leg. "Answer my questions and I won't kill him ... not yet anyway." He flashed her a dark smile.

Kaleus thought about his questions. He didn't want her to know that he couldn't remember Oberon or what he had done, so he needed to choose his words carefully. "Tell me about Oberon ... and you. Were you close?"

Jaika made a gagging noise. *He thinks I liked Oberon. Nobody liked Oberon, except maybe Davin or the other soldiers.*

"I see." Kaleus didn't need an answer. He had scattered bits of information about Jaika being sent to kill Merith, the battle at the mines, and the Breen, but he was interested in what his soldiers didn't know. "Oberon taught you how to enter the castle and kill Merith." It wasn't a question.

Jaika nodded, not understanding that Kaleus did not know Oberon's plans. "Yes. I used the secret door to the prayer room in the back of the castle."

Kaleus paused for a moment, soaking in the information. *Maybe I can use that later,* he thought. *A secret door.*

"But failed," he said, "obviously."

"He recognized me," she answered.

"After all this time?" He knew she had been sent away as a child, but not where she had lived. Only that Oberon had brought her back. Nela had been … helpful with information.

"Yes. He said I looked like my mother."

"Perhaps." Kaleus had seen her mother only from a distance, other than the day his raiders had killed her in one of the markets. They had burned Galimar to the ground, yet he had still risen to take down ten more of his men. "Why attack the mines?" Kaleus wanted to understand her father's plan. "Merith doesn't need crystals."

Jaika didn't answer. He seemed to think Palon sat on a huge deposit of crystals. *Why would he think that?* She thought about his question for a moment. "To free the prisoners." She looked into his eyes with defiance. "The people you worked and tortured."

"So not for the crystals ... just the people?" Kaleus thought she was lying so he traced a line across Richard's leg with the point of his knife. "Just for the people?"

"Yes ... yes ... and to end your army."

Kaleus rubbed his beard and looked past her. "Clever," he mumbled. "And you asked the Breen to fight for you?"

"I don't know why they came." She shook her head no. "I don't know how to speak with them, and I don't know why they came. They seemed to know we were in trouble." She gritted her teeth. "Maybe they don't like you keeping prisoners."

She gripped the handle of her knife for courage. "It's wrong to keep prisoners ... to work men as slaves."

"Yeesss," Kaleus growled. "You should have that discussion with your father. He is the one who taught me."

"You're lying," Jaika snapped, but the memory of the caged prisoners burned in her brain.

Kaleus pushed up the sleeve of his shirt to expose his bare forearm. He folded the cuff into even sections watching the princess with each movement, then made a fist. In scattered places along his arm, the skin shuttered and flipped to become tiny flecks of golden armor. "My mother was half Benjee. She was kicked to the streets by her family because she was not pure. My father found her ... used her to clean his house, cook his meals, and whatever else he wanted. When I was born, he knew I would be like her. So, he hated both of us." His eyes grew cloudy. "One day ... he killed her ... and then I killed him."

Jaika watched his face and mouth as he spoke looking for lies and half-truths, but there was only indifference.

"When I was old enough, I traveled to Palon to become a soldier. I wanted to fight for the righteous King Merith ... offering my life for justice and freedom. But when Keshar saw my gold ... my Benjee markings ... Merith had me imprisoned." He glared at

Jaika. "Your mighty father had me thrown in prison because of my skin."

She hugged the wall. *He's lying,* she told herself. *None of this is true.*

"There were others there, little princess. Others who did not look like ... *him*. Others with gold skin, blue skin, even a man with four arms and one born with only one eye. I had never seen such things ... such people."

Kaleus stood, looking down at Jaika. "That is why I fight, little princess. They rotted in those cells until I helped them escape. I made friends with the guard. Jos ... he helped us. He stayed with me and now he will help me take everything from that fake ... from your father."

Kaleus smiled at the thought of vengeance. "He will pay for what he's done."

Jaika looked down at the floor and tried not to think of the strange looking people imprisoned beneath her father's castle.

Home

This would be the final portal according to Syman. Four doorways he said. Ilea didn't question his calculations. He had been right about so many other things. She was exhausted, but she would find the strength to open one more doorway. Manipulating the SolStone was easier each time she used it. Limiting her connection was the trickiest part. If she became excited, or frustrated, or simply pushed her lifesong too deeply into the SolStone, the results were always a loss of control. She fought the sickening feeling that she could send them all to the place that Nick and Jack called home if she wasn't careful.

Ilea smiled at the red moon as she took her position sitting in the sand. With each trip through the light, the moon had grown larger and higher in the sky. There was no doubt they were getting closer to home. The people waited behind her watching the doorway spiral and open outward. It opened wider than the time before. Her skill was growing, even the travelers could see it.

Syman

One by one the people walked through the portal, carrying their packs and bags. Syman stayed behind, watching the very last person pass through the doorway. Then, as he had done for each doorway, he reached down and gently lifted Ilea from the ground to carry her through the final portal. When they reached the other side, Syman could see Palon etched against the horizon beneath the glow of the red moon. He helped Ilea stand and the watery doorway behind them disappeared.

Now that Palon was in sight, the caravan moved more quickly. The people were driven on by hope and the vision of the city in the distance. Rilo and Kilp stopped to shake hands with Syman before they broke from the group to head for the city of the Benjee beyond Palon and the forest.

Ilea stood staring at the city and the red moon and the people leaving her behind.

"You did well," Syman nodded to Ilea. "We are almost to the city."

But as he spoke, Ilea had stopped looking at Palon. Instead, she was looking at the mountains just beyond. "That's my home," she smiled, "not the city."

"Then you must go." Syman spoke with understanding. "Go and find your family."

Syman

Ilea nodded, "Thank you for your help." She began to remove the strap that held the SolStone around her neck.

"Keep it." Syman put his hand on the stone. "You may need it."

"No," she shook her head. "I will come for it later ... if I need it ... after."

"Yes," Syman agreed. "After."

Ilea backed away, twisting her body sideways and opening her wings to lift from the ground. She flew above the caravan to find Jack and Nick leading the travelers alongside Zaldi and Luna. She dropped to the sand to land in front of her friends.

Nick was beaming with pride. "That's such a great trick," he said. "Opening the doorway." *I can't wait to study one of those crystals. And to think I was wearing a bracelet made of them all these years*

Ilea nodded sadly.

"You're leaving, aren't you." Nick could see the worry in her face.

She turned and pointed to the mountain. "My home. I need to go ... for a while. I need to find my mother, my brother, and ... maybe ..." She couldn't

205

bring herself to say father. "Go to King Merith and find your Jaika. Show her the beads."

She moved closer and wrapped her arms around him. Her wings stretching out behind her, twitching with excitement. Then, almost bouncing on her tiptoes, she hugged Jack as well. "I will find you both," she shouted as she turned and ran. "I promise."

Ilea lifted from the ground. Jack and Nick watched her silhouette cross the red moon.

"At least we did one good thing." Jack grinned. "We got Ilea home."

"We are going to find Jaika too." Nick looked at his friend. "I feel it in my bones."

"I hope your bones are right," Jack agreed. "And I hope this Palon place has some real food. A cheeseburger maybe … or some french fries. I really miss french fries."

Ilea flew toward the mountains. Her exhaustion had been replaced with zeal. She had not been this close to home in such a long time. She could feel the lifesong in the mountains. The low moan of the rocks, the slither of the ground creatures, but most of all she could feel the life in her city. The glorious hum of life. Ilea stretched out her wings and flew as fast as they would carry her.

Syman

As she reached the city, she could feel her home. Dodgen and her mother and ... someone else. Her heart rejoiced, and she spun, rising and falling with joy.

She landed in the sunroom, falling, clawing at the walls. Dodgen heard her first. He came running from inside almost knocking her off the edge of the platform. He rolled her over with a hug.

"You're back! You're back!" he shouted. "That ol' slimy Bartok brought you back."

"No," Ilea shook her wings and folded them closed. "I did it myself. I have so much to tell you." She put her hands on his face looking deep into his eyes. "You'll never believe what I have seen."

"She's home!" He yelled, falling backward. His short wing twitching, folding beneath him.

Seela was next to appear. Falling to her knees in the doorway. Her body weary and thin. Ilea could feel her frailty now that she was close.

"Mother," she wailed, rushing to her side, each wrapping their arms around the other.

"You came back." Seela almost cried. "I don't care how ... I thought I would never see you again." The tears burned her cheeks.

Syman

"I have so much to tell you, mother. So many people we didn't know about. Worlds we didn't know about."

Seela smiled. The weariness tugging at her eyes.

"You can rest now. No more worrying. I'm back, and there are others."

From behind Seela, inside her home, Ilea could feel a presence unlike any she had ever felt before. It was not man nor woman. It was not Tal or Benjee or any other ground dweller. It was not like Nick or Jack. This creature held more knowledge and power than any she had ever encountered.

She felt it move toward the doorway, and as it passed through, her heart stopped. It was Adolphus. She could see her father standing in front of her. His face, his muscled body and wings, but it was not him. Except for the gray of his eyes, every part of this creature's physical body, including the scar that ran from beneath his arm to his stomach was her father, but he was no longer inside. This shell, this blue-skinned body was his, but something else had taken control.

Ilea reached for his lifesong. Pain, agony, anger, fear ... ages and ages of emotions and knowledge. So many lifetimes ... time beyond time. She began to whimper and shake. She freed herself from her mother's embrace, stepped back to the edge of the platform, and dove.

"Ilea!" Dodgen yelled.

Adolphus stepped to the ledge, slowly extended his wings and then lifted from the mountainside. He knew where she would go. To her place, that jagged rock where she went to think, so there was no need to rush. His wings pushed the air as he rose and forced Seela backwards.

Adolphus took his time, rising above the cliffs, following the tops of the mountains to the jagged outcrops where Ilea liked to think she could hide. He landed just above her, watching. Ilea felt his power like a pending storm.

I will not harm you, he thought to her.

"Who are you?" she yelled. "Where is my father? All of my father?"

Adolphus rose again, landing closer to Ilea. "I am Krill." The creature shifted his feet to get a better hold on the rocks. "He is with me. I am here. We are here." He knew it would be difficult for her to understand. "He was dying and beyond my help. So, I joined with him ... to save him."

"You saved my father?" Ilea quivered. She thought about the night at the crystal mines when the soldiers tried to kill them all. The rifle burns tearing into his body. She remembered dragging him across the sand, screaming to his lifesong to stay … to heal. And the mist. The mist that comes with death, when a lifesong leaves the body. "How can any of him still be alive?"

"Kayz saved him … he used the crystals stolen from the wagon. It was enough power to hold his lifesong in place until I could get to him." Adolphus … the creature relaxed his shoulders. "He is here … with me … and he loves you. More than life, he loves you."

"Can I speak to him?" Ilea whispered, her lips trembling.

The gray in his eyes subsided to reveal the water-blue color she knew so well.

"Father?" she breathed. Ilea could feel his body weaken the instant his eyes cleared.

"Lee … I am here."

In that moment, she understood. If that thing left him, he would die. As long as it was inside him, his body would continue … and the mist of his lifesong would stay.

"I love you." Ilea's voice cracked. "I am sorry I couldn't save you."

Adolphus smiled. "But you did save me. Now … there is work to be done."

She didn't understand. She wanted to ask a million questions, but his heartbeat was slowing. He couldn't survive much longer without the other creature … the Krill. The water-blue of his eyes disappeared. His lifesong surged as the gray eyes of the Krill returned.

"Your people will listen to your father. I need his help."

"Who are you?" Ilea felt angry and frustrated and ached to have her father back.

"I am the Krill who guards this planet. I am Levek. I was two, but I am one again."

Ilea frowned at the riddles in his explanation.

"I have lived in the caves of your mountains and in the Palace in Devant. I sing to Palon and the Tal and the Benjee … the trees and the mountains and the sand. But now your world is dying. The Makers were careless."

Ilea growled low and turned her back toward Adolphus. This creature spoke nonsense, but he did have control over her father. She would need time … time to plan. She would need to free her father from this creature.

"We must warn the people of Regar. Help is coming. They must prepare." Adolphus tried again to reason with her.

This Krill will use my father to speak with the Tal. To convince the others ... to make them believe that Regar is dying. How can a mountain die?

Adolphus lifted his shoulders and extended his wings outward. "The people must prepare."

Ilea winced. *What if he is telling the truth?* She wanted time to think. *Maybe Nick will know what to do.*

"In Palon a battle is raging. Many will die if we do not intervene."

Ilea shook her head. "I am home now. I don't want to go to Palon." She knew she should care about those people. Nick and Jack would be in that city and Luna and Zaldi and Syman. They would all be in Palon. They could all die if this Adolphus spoke the truth.

Adolphus looked down at her with suns and suns of patience. "We can help them. You can help them. Whatever they fight for will mean nothing when the world breaks apart. You must make them understand. Help is coming."

Ilea flexed her wings and stood ready to fly. "Who is coming?"

Butcher Boxes

Jaika awoke to a hard kick to her side. Her muscles groaned as she worked to untangle her stiff arms and legs. She had spent the night on the floor next to Richard's bed. Uric placed a bowl of bread and something slimy to eat within her reach. Jaika knew she should kick it aside in case it was poison, but she was starving. Poison was a risk she was willing to take.

"Can I give him some?" She pointed toward Richard.

Uric grunted and shrugged, which Jaika took to mean yes. "And maybe some water?" She tried for more.

Uric pointed to a pitcher on a rickety wooden table in the corner of the room. Then he folded his arms and leaned against the wall to watch her and Richard and the road visible through the open window.

Jaika picked up the bowl, stretched her neck, then stood. Her legs shook, and her heart failed as she realized her knife was gone. *Kaleus must have taken it while*

I was asleep. She gathered her strength, retrieved the pitcher, and made her way to the bed to sit beside Richard. She poured a few drops of water onto her fingers then pressed them to his lips.

"Wake up," she whispered. "You have to wake up." She tore a piece from her cloak and soaked it with water, then used it to clean the blood from his face and head.

Richard moaned and tried to speak. His eyes were swollen and bruised black, but he managed to open them both. Jaika put more water on his lips to force him to drink. He licked the droplets from her fingers then grunted as he tried to lift his head.

"Be still," Jaika soothed. "You need your strength." *I need you to be strong.*

She pinched off part of the bread and dipped it into the soup. Then nibbled the corner to see if the taste was as bad as it looked. Surprisingly, it tasted like Mattie's oatmeal. So she fed some to Richard along with more water. Jaika hadn't lied. Richard would need his strength when Kaleus got back.

They spent the day resting and listening to soldiers reporting and asking questions. Uric barked orders and men came and went until the sun dropped low in the sky. He even fed them again later in the day, which kept Jaika wondering why he bothered to keep them both alive.

Then, Kaleus returned. Three soldiers followed him into the room, including the tall bearded man and Davin. Each carried oddly shaped bags.

"There's so many people outside." Uric had been watching out the window all day.

"The celebration continues." Kaleus sat down on the corner of the bed, took off one boot, and shook it while the sand and pebbles sifted out. "No one will notice us in the crowds. We can go anywhere."

"So, what happens now?" Jos had closed the door and leaned against it.

"Pass out the rest of the butcher boxes. Make sure the men have what they need to hide them." Kaleus said, looking over at Richard now sitting on the floor beside Jaika. "I am glad to see you are feeling better."

Richard glared at the old king. His head hurt and his vision blurred, but he would fight this man to the death.

Jos rubbed his eyes with exhaustion. "The men have their boxes. Most are in position already."

Syman

"What do you have left for the castle?" Kaleus had lost track of the count.

"We have seven."

Kaleus chuckled. "Take one of the seven and wrap it ... a gift fit for a king."

"But how?" Jos shook his head growing tired of the plan.

"There's a nice old lady down in the tavern." Uric smiled. "I bet she'd be glad to help ... for a price."

"Take care of it, then." Kaleus stood. "You two, get up off the floor. You have work to do." He stared at Richard and Jaika then back at the door.

Richard stood with Jaika's help, looking worn and defeated. He leaned against her slim frame and tried not to fall over.

Kaleus couldn't help but laugh, a long, deep, belly laugh. "This is Merith's finest." He laughed again. "Well ... soldier ... it's time to go."

Uric opened the door and the others followed. He motioned for the bearded man to pick up the bags, then they all moved down the dingy hallway. Kaleus kept Richard and Jaika in front of him. Shoving them both when they dragged their feet. Jaika could feel Davin's glare burning through the back of her head.

Syman

Jos caught up with them quickly carrying the wrapped gift, then Kaleus, along with his men and prisoners, walked through the city streets unnoticed. Merchants or customers or revelers, no one cared.

"For six suns they will celebrate," Kaleus spoke low as they walked, leaning forward between Jaika and Richard to make sure they could hear. "Merith will host his private revelry on the final evening. Only acceptable people will be invited." Kaleus focused on Jaika as he explained. His eyes full of hatred. "No commoners … or people like us. His guards will see to that."

Jaika had a vague memory of the grand parties in the castle. The bright-colored clothes and hats and the smells of food and wine and people. Some even wore masks. She had no idea the celebrations were exclusive, that the castle was locked. There were so many people, she thought everyone in the world had been there.

The bearded man left the group with several of the bags. Jaika could only assume he had more weapons to hide. If she could just get word to Keshar or Galimar, they would know what to do.

As they moved closer to the castle, Jaika could see the small rock houses and tents that crowed the road. The same houses she had passed the night she came to kill Merith. There was the restaurant where she had left her saktar and the tent of the fortune teller. The clearing and the smooth wall of the castle lay just beyond.

They stopped in the shadows. Jos took one of the empty bags and placed a single butcher box inside. He held the box in the air as he worked, shifting it side to side, making sure Jaika and Richard knew what was inside the bag. Then he moved closer to tie it around Jaika's waist. He jerked the straps tight and knotted the loose ends to make sure it stayed in place. Jaika could feel his dirty fingers against her back.

"You know," Jos looked at Richard as he finished, "I have a detonator, but a burn gun works just as well."

Even with the pain that wracked his skull, Richard remembered all too well how easy it was to set off a butcher box. Jaika could do it herself if she shook it too hard.

Kaleus held up three fingers in front of Jos and motioned toward the other soldiers. Jos pulled out three of the final butcher boxes from his bag and handed them to Uric as instructed. His hands did not even shake as he hid them in his pack. It would be up to them to find a place for each explosive. Support beams in the lower parts of the castle. His men knew what to do. The other explosives in the city would be denotated after the castle fell. That would be their signal. They had talked it over so many times that Kaleus dreamed about it. The rumbling of the detonations, the blinding light, the smell of charred flesh, and most importantly, the stones in the upper levels collapsing on top of Merith, covering him, smothering him, sealing him beneath the cold rock forever.

At the edge of the city, the men waited with their explosives alongside Kaleus, Richard, and Jaika. Richard stood beside her in the shadows, watching her and Jos and waiting for a chance to strike. Five of the butcher boxes would be planted in the castle. Another sixteen were being scattered about the city. Homes and families would be destroyed without warning. Jaika's stomach knotted and twisted with the thought. Children, fathers, mothers … people who had never offended Kaleus would die. Her life … Richard's life … even her father's life seemed so small against the damage the butcher boxes would cause.

"Now," Kaleus shoved Richard forward. "Lead us to the hidden door in the back of the castle."

Richard looked at Jaika. He knew he should let them kill her. If they both died here, Kaleus would never find the door to the prayer room and into the castle. He would be forced to fight the guards. It was the right thing to do. Keshar would have called it the proper strategical action, but he wasn't here. He didn't have to watch her die and know that he could have saved her. Richard did not have the heart or the courage to let Jaika go. So, he reasoned that if he waited, there would be a chance to stop them. If he stopped Kaleus from setting off the butcher boxes in the castle, the others would not be detonated. His men would wait for a signal that never came.

Richard stepped to the edge of the clearing to study the highest parts of the castle. A pair of Merith's soldiers patrolled the walkway across the upper wall that connected the watch towers. They paced back and forth while Richard counted their steps.

"One, two, three … ten … twenty," he counted until their shadows passed behind the corner tower.

Richard nodded toward Kaleus, and together, they sprinted out into the clearing and across to the stone wall of the castle.

"Gently now my dear." Jos pushed Jaika out into the clearing.

She stiffened her back and held her hand across her waist to keep the box from bouncing as they hurried, side by side, to join Richard and Kaleus against the castle wall. Uric and Davin followed them into the deep shadows. Here, the guards above would never see them.

"Quit stalling, Bartok." Kaleus growled low.

Richard took a deep breath and began edging his way toward the door. The stones of the wall were worn smooth with time, but Richard could feel the cracks filled with mortar that held them in place. He ran his fingers along the cracks feeling for the shift in the design. The bolt, the door, the archway blended so perfectly with the stone that it could be more easily felt than seen. Vines striped the wall and did their best to hide Merith's secret. But soon enough, his fingers felt the archway that marked the entrance into the lower level … into Merith's prayer room … and eventually his bedroom. Richard slid the bolt open that held the door.

With the latch open, Richard motioned to Kaleus to go inside, but the old king just smiled and patted his gun. "After you my young soldier."

Richard turned back toward the door and tried one more time to think of a plan to save them all, but the thought of Jaika next to that butcher box was all he could see. He gritted his teeth, then pushed open the door. The others quickly followed. The final soldier pulled the door closed with only a click of the bolt to break the silence.

In the blackness, Jaika pictured the hallway in her mind. The number of steps to the prayer room were etched in her memory, but even in there she wouldn't be safe. She thought about the night she had walked this hallway alone, feeling her way along the wall, careful not to make a sound. But tonight was different. Tonight, she wanted to scream and yell and tell whoever might be listening that they were here. But she knew that no matter how much noise she made, there would be no one in the prayer room to hear. Everyone would be at the celebration. No one will know what is coming.

A flash of light tore open the darkness as Kaleus lit one of the torches that hung on the wall. As the fire grew, Richard could see what was left of a burn round from Kaleus's gun melting and dripping from the edge of the torch. If he didn't hate Kaleus so much, he would have asked him to teach him that fire-lighting trick.

"Well," Kaleus snarled as he lifted the torch from the wall, "let's get on with it."

Jaika nodded to Richard. She hoped he understood that she trusted him and would follow whatever he had planned.

Richard led the way down the dusty hall past the planked prayer room door. Jaika couldn't help but count the steps as they passed. Her mind filled with images of the alter and the statues and her father and the night she had come to take his life. The hallway ended with a series of short steps leading down into yet another hallway. She remembered the moldy smell when she had walked this way with Keshar. He had thought she was a man. That night felt like a lifetime ago.

They continued to follow the twists and turns in the hallway until it ended with a wall of stairs. Steep stairs with a doorway at the top that led to Merith's bedroom.

Kaleus gripped Richard by the shoulder. "Jos will come behind her with his burn gun. You try something and ..."

"I know," Richard jerked away, "I know." He tried not to think about the butcher box and what it could do to her.

He climbed the steps hoping that Merith and Keshar would be there, at the top, making plans in Merith's chambers. But in his heart, he knew they were at the celebration. Everyone was at the celebration. No one would hear the creaking cabinet door or the rustling of clothes as Richard entered. It was up to him to save Jaika.

At the top, he wove his hand through the hanging clothes to push open the cabinet door. He climbed from the top step and out into Merith's room, disappointed that it was empty. Kaleus emerged from the cabinet after Richard followed closely by Davin. Richard growled as Davin turned back to help Jaika out of the cabinet, then smiled when she shoved his hand aside. Her eyes burned with hatred.

"Remember," Kaleus could see Richard watching for Jos to appear from inside the cabinet … watching for a chance to escape. "I have a burn gun too."

Richard took a step back to show that he understood.

Jos stepped out of the cabinet then ran his fingers down Jaika's cloak. He stopped at the bulge along her waist. "Still there I see."

Richard bit back the urge to smash the man's face.

"Pitiful room," Kaleus muttered, tired of waiting for the others. "Merith is not much of a king. He lives in squalor like his people."

"Soon it won't matter," Jos sneered. "There won't be any kingdom left."

Kaleus snorted. "No kingdom at all." He savored the idea of the castle crumbing around them, then motioned toward Richard. "Look out in the hallway."

Uric stood beside Richard as he opened the door to peer out into the empty hallway. "No one is there." Richard assured Kaleus, wishing it wasn't true. "They must all be at the celebration.

Jos turned to search the cabinet they had used as a door. "We are going to look out of place in here. Those people will be in their finest, or even in disguise." He pulled a soft red tunic and velvet cape from the hanging clothes and tossed them to Kaleus. "These should fit you nicely."

Uric shrugged and chuckled, "And what have you for me, my Lord?"

Jos took out two more tunics in purple and blue and held them up for the others to see. He smiled at Jaika as they robbed her father's room. "Good thing your father is not a fat man."

Jaika bit back the words she wanted to say.

Kaleus studied Richard's bloody face and clothes then pointed toward a table with a basin of water. "Clean him up, girl. No one will believe that face is a part of a costume."

225

Jaika led Richard over to the table and used a cloth and water to clean the blood from his face. "I can't fix your eyes," she whispered. Her hand shaking as she worked.

Kaleus snapped, "Enough! He looks like the back end of a saktar."

Jos took out another cape and a white scarf. "Use this to cover his face. Wrap his head like someone from the sand."

Jaika did her best to create a proper covering that ended with a tail to cover his mouth. He put on the cloak and Richard was no more. He was just a wealthy traveler.

Jos handed a second scarf to Kaleus. "You need to cover your face as well. They will recognize you."

Kaleus nodded and made himself into a sand traveler.

Uric took out a soft green tunic from the cabinet and tossed it at Davin. "No one will know your face. They won't care that you are here." Uric didn't say that he hated Davin, but his words made it clear enough. "But, there's nothing here for her." Uric raised an eyebrow. "I would have liked to put her in a very special costume."

Syman

Richard stepped toward the man, but Jaika gripped his arm. "I will keep my cloak up over my face. No one will see me."

"It will have to do." Kaleus looked at Uric and Jos. "Keep your weapons ready but out of sight."

"And if she runs?" Jos asked with a grin.

"Kill them both," Kaleus smiled, "but stand back so that the butcher box doesn't kill you." Then he laughed, dark and cold and unforgiving.

Jos and Uric laughed too, but Jaika didn't think any of this was funny. Uric opened the door and they walked out into the empty hallway.

Richard led the men down the empty hallways toward the laughter and music of the celebration. In the dining hall, the tables had been pushed closer to the walls and most were covered with food. This left an open space in the middle for dancing. Six men sang in harmony as others around the room joined in on stringed instruments. The crowd clapped and laughed and circled in dance. Merith sat at the front, elevated on a platform.

Jaika found herself wondering why they were celebrating the sun. *The sun never changes. It looks the same all the time. So, what is a new sun?* She would ask Richard later when they had less to worry about.

Jos slipped Kaleus the wrapped package and the detonator then motioned with his head toward one of the serving boys. Kaleus nodded in agreement. He flashed a sliver of white crystal toward the boy to call him over. The boy could not have known that the package Kaleus handed him contained a butcher box. The instructions were clear, and for the price of a grain of white crystal, the boy would carry it and a short note to King Merith. He would personally present it to the king so that the gift would not be lost or mixed with any others. The boy grinned, pocketed the crystal shard, and carried the package away.

The men exchanged nods, then Uric and Jos disappeared into the castle to begin hiding the rest of the butcher boxes. Kaleus pointed to Davin who was more than happy to stand guard over Richard – the man who had pretended to be his friend.

"Remember," Kaleus gripped Richard and Jaika by the shoulder to pull them close. "I don't have to be standing beside you to activate the detonator."

Jaika swallowed hard and wondered just how far away she would have to be before the others were safe.

Kaleus decided on a vantage point in the far corner of the main hall. Davin followed, shoving Richard and Jaika toward the back of the room, and sticking his burn gun into Richard's back.

"Give me a reason to kill you … please." Davin begged Richard. "I owe you a thousand deaths."

"I had to lie to save her." Richard tried to explain. "It was nothing personal."

"You lied to me." Davin pushed them both beyond the tables and chairs and dancers. "Just like everyone else."

They made their way through the chatting, drinking, self-righteous guests to the back corner behind a statue of a soldier in full armor. Here, Kaleus relaxed. This was his time to enjoy. He wanted to watch the guests, the soldiers, and most of all, Merith. He wanted to relish his time waiting for the right moment. The moment Merith opened the gift and knew his time was over. Time … there was plenty of time to wait. He had waited so long already. This was his moment to savor. The time of Merith's destruction.

Costumes

As the caravan of travelers entered the city of Palon, Oberon started making plans. He knew that Syman would soon revert to his two-legged form, and his crippled leg would once again be his only method of transportation. So, moving around the city wouldn't be easy. Still, there was more to do while he was here than just move around. This might be the last chance he would ever have to face Merith.

Syman's body shimmered, and Oberon slid to the ground. His bags fell into a crumpled mound behind them. Once the transformation from saktar to man was complete, Syman paused to get his bearings. The city, the red moon, and the travelers dispersing behind him. He watched Oberon as he swung his crippled leg beneath him in a rhythmic swaying pattern, trudging across the ground to disappear into the city. Then he looked behind him to see one of the bags was open and the soft cloth inside that had held the SolStone was empty.

Syman

Luna slid from Zaldi to walk beside Jack. She tucked her clothing around her body to cover her light, but in the darkness her face glowed from beneath her scarf. Nick and Syman walked beside them both. Zaldi's broad shoulders towering over the others.

"I will stay close to you," Luna whispered in Jack's ear. "You look like one of them."

Jack repeated her words to Syman for translation, but he mangled most of them.

"I'm not sure," Syman did his best, "but I think she said that you look like a man from Palon."

Jack scratched his head and squinted toward the city. He had never considered the idea that he looked like a person from another world. Aliens were supposed to be green and have big eyes. But, then again, he was the alien in this place.

As they walked into the city, they immediately drew curious stares and threats. Luna's fingers dug into Jack's arm, but he didn't mind.

"Freaks!"

"You don't belong here!"

"I'll show you what we do with people like you!"

A red fruit struck Syman in the shoulder and a stone hit Zaldi in the side. Nick and Jack did not understand their shouts, but it was clear they were not friendly.

Syman shimmered and hazed to change into the dragon. He spread his wings, threw back his head, and breathed out a roar that shook the air. Then he hazed again to return to his man-form.

"We are part of the festival!" Syman yelled out to the quivering crowd. "We are here to entertain!"

Nick could hear the crowd gasp then their hushed murmurs that rose and fell. Suddenly, the crowd began to cheer and clap. The travelers' differences were now seen as costumes and makeup. Now, they were actors instead of … freaks. Syman had protected them, as always.

The crowd soon lost interest and returned to talking and working and drinking and whatever tasks filled their night. Most of the caravan scattered, pulling their cloaks over their heads to disappear into the crowds. They had families and friends to find. Those who had been brought to the Lost City by the Breen … those who had escaped the mines or been left to die in the sand would be welcomed as a ghost returning from the dead. It would be a joyous time for their families. The two Benjee boys had already fled as well as Oberon, leaving only five members of the caravan behind.

Syman

"I want to find Jaika," Nick told Jack as they watched the others leaving.

Syman overheard. "You must seek her in Merith's castle, in the center of the city."

"That ought to be easy enough to find." Jack patted Luna's hand still gripping his arm.

They walked together into the city. Zaldi watching over the top of the crowds for danger. Syman announcing their arrival as performers if the crowds became unfriendly. Zaldi would kneel and wave and pretend he liked the attention. Together, they wove their way past the market tents to the inner parts of the city, past homes and stony houses toward the castle … Jaika's castle … standing tall in the center, shimmering in the darkness.

"The castle may be blocked today because of the Festival of the New Sun," Syman explained as they moved closer to its stone walls.

"What the heck is the new sun?" Jack snapped. "The sun doesn't change … does it?"

Syman stopped to stare at Jack. "Our planet orbits a sun, as do many planets. According to the Maker's data, there are two junctures at which the time with the sun and the time without are the same. The following days, our time with the sun will grow longer or shorter each time it crosses the sky until it reaches its peak."

"The solstice … the day and night are the same length." Nick began to understand.

"After this juncture, our time with sunlight will decrease slightly after each rising and setting of the sun," Syman continued.

"This would be the summer solstice with shorter days leading the planet toward winter." Nick pushed at his glasses. "So, the days will get colder?"

"Yes," Syman agreed. "The nights will see a change in temperature as well."

"So, we are going to have more hot days?" Jack whined. "When does winter get here?"

Nick shrugged. "I don't think this place has an extreme winter. Maybe the temperature is basically consistent. There are places on Earth like that. I would have to study the orbit and the …"

"Ahhhhh!" Jack moaned. "I get it. The days are always hot. Let's just go to the castle."

"To the castle it is. What do you think, Syman?" Nick asked. "Do you think the guards would accept us as part of the show? Would that get us into the castle?"

Syman

"Perhaps." Syman thought about Nick's question. "It *is* a festival of costumes."

"This festival," Nick was intrigued, "does it date back to the time of the Makers?"

"Yes," said Syman. "The Makers believed this was a holiday celebrated on many worlds. "Holidays boost morale … give workers a time to rest."

"I have always liked a good holiday," Jack mused as they started walking again.

"Our people are quite unique … Zaldi and Luna especially." Syman returned his focus on getting them into the castle. "Perhaps with some additional clothing we could pass as performers."

"Keep your eyes open." Jack shook his finger at the rest of their group. "We need additional clothing." Then he lowered his voice to a whisper. "Because we are not already hot enough."

Only the quickest eyes would have seen Syman as he stole a red cloak and a wide hat with a feather and rainbow-colored scarf from the market tables as they walked. He would pass them to the others with instructions in a language Nick and Jack could not understand. The travelers were quickly covered in gaudy, bright-colored clothes and could pass for whatever they needed to be to gain entrance to the castle.

Soon, they walked beneath the castle wall with its great arched doorways. Soldiers dotted the top of the wall, watching everyone who came or went. Nick could feel a change in the city as they cleared the gates. The structures were more permanent and better maintained. The tents were in groups and made of durable fabric with less tears and stains. More money, more safety, something made this area more affluent.

Closer to the castle, the number of guards increased. Several stopped to speak with Syman who soon had them pointing and giving directions to the side entrance. Information that performers would need to know.

Nick felt like he had traveled back in time, on Earth, to the medieval era. Except here … Syman appeared to be a robot and the people in the Lost City were unlike any other creatures. They had two-way mirror tents and Ilea could create an Einstein-Rosen bridge with her mind and a stone. Earth didn't have any of these things. *So, is this the past or the future for this place? How can they live so primitively and yet have such advancements?*

Syman watched Nick trying to understand his surroundings. "The stone of the castle," Syman explained, "absorbs the sunlight to make it glow."

"Solar, of course." Nick nodded. The cause of the castle light had not even crossed his mind.

"The rock can help to provide light inside the castle and warmth when needed. The properties of the stone are a variation on the stone in Ilea's necklace."

"The crystals," Nick said. "They are very important to your planet."

"Yes. Without them the planet would cease to produce water and food. The different colored crystals have different functions. Some processes require more than one color crystal."

Nick thought about the stones Syman had used to make water in the desert. "They can merge hydrogen and oxygen to create water ... H_2O."

"I do not understand." Syman continued walking toward the side of the castle.

"Don't worry about it," Nick answered. He was pretty sure there wasn't any chemistry classes on this planet.

Guards were lined up at the side entrance to the castle when they arrived. No one was allowed to enter without extensive questioning. Some guests displayed a ring or pendant with special markings that allowed them entry. As they waited their turn, the guards stared and pointed at Zaldi. Luna tried to keep her face covered, but in the darkness, it was almost impossible. She still held onto Jack as if he were invincible.

Syman took his turn to speak with the main guard. "We have been asked to come and perform for the king."

"I can't let you in." The guard held up his hand to push Syman back. "These are Keshar's orders. You must have a seal or written permission. You were not invited."

Syman tried to explain that Zaldi was a unique individual who had traveled a great distant to perform. King Merith had requested their presence. Syman turned and said something to Zaldi in a language the guards could not understand. Zaldi nodded then bent his front legs to lower his body to the ground in a bow.

Syman waved his hands for the half-man, half-saktar to stand. "Your king will be highly displeased if he misses such a chance. Zaldi is quite unique."

The guard looked at the other soldiers, trying to make up his mind.

Suddenly, Syman loosened the tie at the neck of his tunic. The neck opened and dropped to expose his right shoulder. He had a circular mark on his upper arm. A brand, maybe, or a tattoo. Nick couldn't be sure what had made the mark, but he was certain it matched one of the symbols in Ilea's blue stone. The one she had used to open doorways.

"I bear the mark of the Maker."

The guard gasped and stepped away. "That is only a story. No one has this mark."

"And yet, here it is in front of you." Syman showed no sign of emotion or hesitation. Syman was … Syman.

The guard stared at each of them for a moment trying to understand the markings and weighing his options. He even reached out to touch Syman's mark but changed his mind. The guard stepped back, took a deep breath, then yelled out a command that Nick and Jack could not understand. Two new soldiers appeared from the crowds and joined their group. One stood on either side of Syman. Pointing and pushing, they escorted him through the door. Nick and the others were allowed to follow as well. The guards were careful not to come too close to Zaldi.

Jack assessed the situation quickly. "So, we are under house arrest. That didn't take long." Luna patted Jack on the chest, making him feel as invincible as she believed him to be. "Everything is going to be fine," he assured her … and himself. "After all, we are friends with the king's daughter, right?"

"I hope we make it that far." Nick sounded discouraged. "Jaika may not even be here."

"She wouldn't miss her dad's party." Jack winked at Luna even though she didn't understand a single word.

Every head turned as they entered. Zaldi had to duck his head to pass through several doorways. Luna pulled her cloak about her body, but the glow of her skin escaped from between the folds of fabric. Zaldi, however, refused to hide. Unafraid of anyone, he held his head high and thrust out his chest in defiance. His feet plodding against the stone floor.

The soldiers led them down a long hallway to a room filled with people and racks of clothes and scarves and hats. As they entered, all motion stopped. The performers stopped dressing and backed away from the door with their mouths wide open, frozen, waiting for someone, anyone to move first. Even in this room, filled with costumes and painted faces, Zaldi and the others were seen as monsters.

Jack, Nick, and Luna stood together in the doorway waiting for Syman to bark an order or explain the next step in the plan. Luna smiled and tried to look non-threatening while holding on to Jack. Zaldi crossed his arms and shifted his feet back and forth. As they looked around the room, Jack patted Luna's hand which filled her with hope that maybe the others in the room would eventually see that she was not dangerous.

Syman said something to the crowd causing everyone to laugh and then, one by one, return to their preparations. The men and women in the room continued painting colors on their faces. One man hooked tall poles to his legs so that he was a giant when he stood. Another tossed glowing orbs that hovered and danced above his fingers.

"Now what?" Jack shrugged.

"We need to get out of here and find Jaika," Nick grumbled. "That's what."

Syman shook his head. "I think we will be forced to perform."

Jack winked at Luna. "Can you sing? Can any of you sing?"

Syman spoke with Luna and Zaldi to come up with a plan. "They will ride in together," Syman translated to English. "Waving and presenting themselves to the king should be sufficient."

"I'm going out there with them," Jack disagreed. "I don't want anything to happen to Luna." *I'm not as big as Zaldi, but I can be helpful. She knows I can be helpful.* Jack studied the racks of clothes. "I bet I can beef up my costume to walk beside a glowing lady and an almost centaur." Jack was proud he had remembered that word.

Trying to avoid any arguments, Syman asked the strangers about the clothes on the wall, but no one claimed ownership. So together, they scavenged the hanging clothes. They would need better disguises if they were to become performers for the king.

Revenge

In time Oberon found his rhythm, using his walking stick to swing and sway and make his way through the city. He knew the shortcuts and the safest routes to the castle. He even managed to steal a curved knife from an unattended table in the market.

He had a plan. He could enter unseen through the secret door hidden in the stone at the back of the castle. The door that led to Merith. The place he had sent Jaika to kill her father. Still, he might never make the climb up the steep stairway to Merith's bedroom. It was the evening of the Celebration of the New Sun. Merith would be in the main hall among the music and revelry. He would be easy enough to find if he could just make the climb.

Closer to the castle, he met a kind man headed to the celebration with a wagon full of supplies. He made space among the baskets for Oberon to sit and rest his legs. The guards welcomed them through the gates and to the side of the kitchen along with the other deliveries. The guards even helped Oberon climb out of the back of the wagon as he carried one of the smaller baskets into the kitchen, swaying and swinging his cane.

He made three trips from the wagon and back into the kitchen with a bag or a basket. The workers in the kitchen were more than kind, offering to carry and lift and do his work for him. The old woman, who had made sandwiches for Jaika, offered him a place to rest and a bite to eat. He tried to say no, but they would not accept his refusal. They found him a place to sit, made him a meal, and began unloading the wagon. Back and forth they walked past him from the kitchen to the wagon and back again, chatting and carrying supplies. His chair was empty when the final bags were unloaded.

A stream of servants carried trays of sweets and drinks and breads through the main door of the kitchen and out into a crowd of laughing people. Oberon wanted to know what was happening, so to blend in, he grabbed a tin with slices of bread from the counter and followed the trail of servants, fighting to control his leg with every step.

They wove their way in and out of the guests until Oberon found a half empty table to rid himself of the bothersome tin. He left the trail of servants to lace his way through the groups of guests, talking and chatting, drinking and eating, clustering along the hallway, oblivious to those who walked past.

Swinging and swaying, he made his way toward the main hall and the music and laughter within. The people he passed saw him as a man in a costume not a cripple with an eyepatch and a cloak and a walking staff. Navigating a path through the river of guests, he entered through the thick wooden doors into the main hall.

"I've returned," he whispered to the ceiling. Then he smiled as he realized there would be no steps to climb after all for Merith sat at the front of the main hall, elevated on his throne to watch his people.

As a Guardian, Oberon would never have been invited to the festival. Guardians were supposed to live without distractions, without possessions, without love, to focus only on Gelquin. But that wasn't the way it had worked. Without love he had grown to hate Gelquin and Merith. Galimar had made sure of that when he tried to destroy the SolStone and betray them all. He would be sure to watch for Galimar as well. *Perhaps I will hide among the crowd and use my knife to kill both of them.* He could feel the hatred flowing through his back and strengthening his limbs.

Toward the back of the room was a second set of doors. People wandered in and out, stopping along the food tables, chatting, dancing, exiting through the other doors, absorbed in the festivities. Oberon took advantage of their distraction to work his way to the back wall. Here he was protected and could look out into the crowd. Leaning his weight against the wall, he relaxed and tried to stretch his crippled leg. He studied Merith and the front platform and the musicians who moved around the room as they sang. Then ... on his left side ...in the back corner of the room ... he saw them. Hiding in the far corner behind a statue of a sword-carrying soldier was Davin, two men with scarf covered faces, and a cloaked figure. Surely, one of these was Kaleus, the red-haired king of Devant.

Oberon held his breath and pulled the hood of his cloak over his head. He stepped away from the wall to hide among the guests. Kaleus or one of his men might recognize him, even with his deformities. He could not afford to get too close ... not just yet.

His mind buzzed with questions as he moved silently. *Why is Kaleus here? And Davin? Maybe Kaleus is here to kill Merith, and Davin is part of the plan.* Oberon smiled beneath his cloak. *This could be a new beginning. Maybe I have been given a second chance. Today I could see Merith destroyed. Today I will tell my son how much I...* He took a deep breath and scolded himself for getting so excited. *It will take time. If Kaleus moves away from his men, I can speak with Daven alone.*

Syman

Suddenly it didn't matter if Kaleus saw him. *Kaleus will never risk detection … even if he recognizes me. He won't move until the perfect time to carry out his plan.* Oberon looked down at his feet and made his way back to the wall where he first had a clear view of the statue and the men behind it. Here he could stand and watch. The old king had a plan, and Oberon would wait to see it carried out. *Kaleus is the perfect weapon.* Chills ran along his arms and legs at the thought of being witness to Merith's fall.

Holding his hood tight against his neck, Oberon slipped closer to the corner where Kaleus hid with Davin and the others. His leg was beginning to ache, so he searched for a place to sit down and rest. The closest seating was a bench that held a round woman balancing a plate stacked high with food. She cradled each piece of bread or meat as though it were a precious jewel. When her plate was empty, and she waddled away toward a serving table, Oberon took her place. His back stiffened and a surge of confidence overcame the last of his fear. He pulled the cloak from his face to expose the scars and eyepatch that covered the Breen's handiwork. If Davin and Kaleus recognized him, they would know his strength and just how difficult it was to kill him. He had the patience of the sand, the patience of a Guardian. He could wait here forever if necessary … wait for his second chance.

Syman

Save the World

Ilea flew to the top of Merith's castle and landed on the one of the highest walls above the guards who paced the open walkways. Thin slits of melted-sand glass lined the upper edges of the wall. A place to let in sunlight. A place only a Tal could reach. The red moon and the glow of the castle threatened to reveal her position, but she was careful ... bouncing from window to window, hiding in the deepest shadows, and feeling the excitement of the people inside. The music rippled along the stone walls and made the melted sand windows pulse with its rhythms. Ilea could feel every beat. Here she would wait until Adolphus and the others arrived.

She found the lifesongs of Jack and Nick and Syman inside the castle. The glowing light from Luna and the restless stomping that was Zaldi. They were apart from the music and chaos of the room below her, but they were safe and inside the castle ... somewhere. The strangers beneath the windows were filled with joy and song and the hazy glow of too much drink, but there was another emotion. Closer to the back of the room, away from the king who sat on the platform. Someone who was not here to enjoy the celebration ... a dark, heavy fear that raged against the music and laughter of the festival. Someone inside the castle was planning destruction.

Ilea paused at the top of the castle to lean against a curved stone wall that surrounded one of the towers. She double checked that no one was watching then closed her eyes and released part of her lifesong into the castle and the city. She wanted to know what was going on.

In the outer city, Ilea could feel the people eating and sleeping and working. They came and went and paid no attention to the people in the castle. They paid no attention to the crystals that hummed within the city. The crystals that made the water in the great river. The bits of white crystal that made their lights and heat. And the vicious fire crystals that were scattered about the city. Volatile, unstable crystals used only for weapons.

Ilea caught her breath and focused her thoughts on the castle. Inside, she could still feel that mix of anger and fear and joy and the same hum of crystals that filled the city. They were so many crystals working in the castle: lights for the celebration, heat for the cooks, and water for the baths. Her lifesong whispered across the stone and the people to reach beneath the castle, along the bones that held it in place. There, she could feel the hum of more fire crystals. The same reckless crystals from the city. She had felt this kind of weapon before. As a child, she had seen the destruction it could unleash. These weapons held the strongest crystals. Crystals that vibrated with energy and fought to be released.

They were everywhere.

She could feel them beneath the castle and scattered about the city. Two were also inside the main hall surrounded by music and laughter. If they all exploded, there would be nothing left of Palon … and nothing left of her friends.

Ilea covered her heart with her hands and opened her eyes. There was no one else who could help these people. She had to stop them. She had to save her friends.

Ilea opened her wings and lifted off from the tower wall to land on the empty lookout platform at the very top of the castle. She settled down behind the half-wall that ran around its edge. She would be vulnerable while she worked. Syman and Jack and Nick would not be here to protect her, so the wall would be her only defense. There, completely hidden from the people, she unfurled her lifesong, sending it to the edge of the city to find the explosive farthest from the crowds in the castle. Beneath a table in a metal merchant's tent was the first butcher box.

This would be nothing like the metal in the shackles she had destroyed to release her brother, or opening a door in the desert, or healing a man with a wounded knee. If she made a mistake, if she was wrong, the crystals inside the weapon would react and destroy everything around them. Instead of targeting the fire crystals, her lifesong sought out the tiny intricate pieces that surrounded the crystals, holding them in place. She could not destroy the crystal without discharging its power, so she focused on those tiny pieces. Her lifesong caressed the metal and the stone that laced together to restrain the crystal. She pressed against each piece, just a twitch, to see what it affected … what else moved inside the weapon. *I wish my father was here. He would know what to do.*

Ilea could feel the fire inside the crystal screaming to get out. The chamber that surrounded it was filled with a cloth padding to prevent the metal from scraping against it. Coils and levers and a sharp blade balanced outside the chamber, waiting to be released, waiting to create a spark that would trigger the fire crystal.

The metal was not pure. Just like the prison shackles, tiny bits of sand and bubbles of air mixed within. Ilea tugged at these impurities with her lifesong. The metal blade beside the crystal began to shudder and crumble. The coil behind it released, rupturing the metal casing, tearing through the cloth padding to hit the fire crystal. Ilea encircled the box with her lifesong making a tube of light that forced the power of the stone upward. Her claws dug into the stone floor of the castle as the crystal burst. Ilea screamed and shook and forced the explosion into the sky. The light tore through the table and the cloth tent top as it shot into the darkness. A white stream of light, silent and quick.

She collapsed against the half-wall of the tower. Tears burned her eyes and her hands shook with fear and anger and pain. The explosive had defeated her. Hopelessness ran across her body like water. She had counted sixteen explosives in the city and more beneath the castle. If one exploded here, she could not hope to channel its power upward through the building and the people. Everyone would die.

Dodgen whispered in her memories. *Stop torturing the rocks.*

Ilea sat up, wiping the tears from her eyes. *Maybe I don't have to destroy anything?* She thought about the doorways she had made in the sand and Syman's words. *Maybe this is not so different. Maybe I need to do what I do best ... heal.*

Syman

She relaxed her shoulders and reached out with her lifesong again. The next explosive was in a stack of wooden crates holding ale for the celebration. People walked past it without knowing it could take their lives at any moment. Ilea whispered to the fire crystal. Her lifesong danced across its surface to feel the jagged edges where it had been torn from the ground. Her light polished and smoothed and sealed the wounds on the outer edges of the stone. She sang as she worked. A healing song just like she had sung to Andy and her father. A shell began to form around the stone. Its edges healing, hardening, weaving together to protect the power within.

Ilea smiled and relaxed her shoulders. Her wings puddled around her on the stone. The crystal was just as powerful as it ever was, but now it would take much more than the metal blade inside the device to break through and release its power. The stone was healed and safe. The butcher box was useless.

Ilea rolled her neck and stretched her arms above her head. Thirteen … fourteen … fifteen boxes … she had lost count. There were so many butcher boxes to stop in the city and then inside the castle. She settled back against the wall, took a deep breath, and went back to work.

The End of Palon

Davin studied the sword that hung from the belt of the statue soldier. "What are we waiting for?" he asked, patting the lump beneath Jaika's cloak along her waist.

"The right time," Kaleus snapped, motioning toward Jaika and Richard. "And keep your hands on them."

Richard glared over at the king.

"We are waiting on the gift," Kaleus continued. "Soon, he will open the gift and then it will be the right time. There's a note inside," Kaleus mused. "When he opens it, he will send everyone away." He smiled at the idea. "He will know I am here. He will know his daughter has been given the same gift. Then it will be time."

Davin listened to Kaleus rant but looked past him at a scarred man with a cane sitting on a bench not too far away. There was something familiar about the man … the way he moved … the way he tilted his head … probably just some old man in a costume.

#

A bony man with a round hat, that looked as though it had been smashed in several places, stepped into the dressing room. Jack and Nick now wore feathers and striped shirts and bright-colored hats. Luna wore a metallic mask that covered her eyes but allowed the glow of her face to shine around it. She sat atop Zaldi, who needed no costume at all.

"It's time for us to perform," Syman translated the bony man's instructions into enough languages so that everybody understood. "Luna will ride atop Zaldi. We will make several turns around the main hall and then leave. That should make them happy."

"Then we can look for Jaika," Nick nodded in agreement.

Jack and Luna also nodded. Zaldi shook back his hair in annoyance.

They followed the bony man down a busy hallway to the main hall. The music stopped, and the guests cheered and gasped as they entered the room. A man on a throne watched from a platform at the front of the hall. Syman, Jack, and Nick followed Zaldi, smiling and waving and trying to look like they were having a good time. Three golden-skinned Benjee boys followed behind them tossing bottles and balls and even knives to each other. Knives that could never penetrate their metallic skin even if they missed.

From behind the statue in the corner of the main hall, Jaika's heart froze. She covered her mouth then reached across Davin to grab Richard's hand. In the center of the room, behind this monster ... this half-saktar half-man, walked Nick and Jack, with ridiculous clothes, and another man she didn't know.

"That's impossible," she whispered to the crowd. *How could they be here? Jack ... Nick... how could they be on Regar? And this monster ... are they his prisoners.*

She squirmed against Davin's grip. He shook her hard and she closed her eyes to wait for the butcher box to fire, but the explosion did not come. Her eyes crept open to watch her friends again, walking and waving and, for an instant, her heart soared with joy. Her friends were here. *Nick will know what to do. Nick will* ... Davin shifted his position. His hip pushed against the butcher box on her waist and the cold truth settled in her bones. *If Kaleus detonates the butcher boxes, Jack and Nick will die.*

Syman

The guests were mesmerized as Zaldi circled the room with Luna waving from his back. The audience paid no attention to the young servant boy Kaleus had paid to deliver his gift to Merith. He was standing at the edge of the platform at the front of the room waiting his turn. He too was intrigued by the half-man, half-saktar.

Kaleus growled with annoyance at the performers. He pushed Davin back against the wall then shoved Richard and Jaika out into the open to get a better view of the king. As he watched, the young boy holding the gift stepped onto the platform near Merith. He placed the gift in the king's hands and then scampered away clutching the crystal shard in his pocket.

Zaldi bowed and Luna swept her glowing arms out in welcome.

Davin held his breath as Merith pulled at the strings that held the cloth wrapping in place. The cloth unfolded in his lap to expose the box. No one in the crowd was watching the king. This was just another gift. Everyone was watching Zaldi.

Merith held the note above the package reading and re-reading each word over and over. Then he motioned for Keshar, Captain of the Guard, to come to his chair. He whispered in the man's ear, then handed him the gift.

Keshar hesitated, backed away from the king, then turned to stroll away as though he carried just another unimportant gift. He left through the front double doors of the main hall and, for a heartbeat, Davin thought nothing would happen. Then the soldiers came. Only a few at a time, ushering guests from the room, whispering excuses. Zaldi and the performers stopped walking to watch two gray-tuniced soldiers guide a fussy old man and a thin lady in a blue dress toward the doors.

"Something's wrong." Jack grabbed Nick by the arm. "Where did all those soldiers come from? And the king has a new guard ... he wasn't there before."

Nick shook his head. "You're right, Jack. Something is going on."

Oberon watched as well. He watched the room full of guests becoming an empty hall. He heard the clatter of instruments as they were carried from the room. Reluctant guests argued and fought with the soldiers who were ruining the celebration. Zaldi and his friends followed the soldiers out into the hallway, but Nick had other plans. He wanted to see what was going on. He pulled off his hat and the striped shirt that covered his worn tunic then merged into the crowd. He made his way to the doors that led to the front of the room beside the platform where Merith sat with his new guards. Nick stood in the doorway beside a battle worn soldier who waited to intervene. Syman and the others waited behind them.

The room was not empty, but Kaleus could no longer wait. He shoved his prisoners closer to the front platform ... closer to Merith. Richard fought to stay by Jaika's side. Davin watched them walk away, then followed, dragging his feet.

Kaleus growled something in another language then jerked the hoods from his prisoner's faces.

"Please," Merith begged, now standing on the platform. "Please do not hurt my daughter."

Oberon smiled from his bench. The king was older and weaker than he remembered. It had been such a long time. And now ... Kaleus had Merith's daughter. This was the perfect plan. She was the perfect weapon against Merith.

"Your butcher box is far away from here by now." Merith tried to reason with his enemy.

"Your daughter has another box," Kaleus said, walking toward the throne, pushing his two captives closer to the king.

Syman

Kaleus reached down to slide open Jaika's cloak and expose the butcher box that hung from her waist.

Jack slugged Nick in the shoulder. "I told you we'd find her." He almost sang the words in the doorway.

Nick jumped and turned to stare at his friend. "She's a prisoner of that crazy man, dufus. We didn't just find her."

Behind Kaleus, the crippled man with an eyepatch stood from his bench and walked toward the center of the room. Merith watched the man hobble and fight to keep his balance. The king could not place the old man's crippled walk or his eyepatch, but still, he knew this man. Somewhere … from the past.

As Oberon neared the others, he could see Keshar beside two young men standing in the hallway outside of the open doors. *Helpless Keshar. You can do nothing to save her. Jaika and your beloved Merith will die. I only wish Galimar could see us now.* As Oberon's hatred grew, the SolStone that hung from a cord around his neck began to warm.

Kaleus stared down at the detonator in his hand. "I do not want your daughter." He looked up at Merith and then glanced over his shoulder at Oberon. "I want … I want … want you to feel pain … to lose everything." Kaleus studied Merith as though he were a stranger.

"Let her go and you shall have everything!" Merith's voice echoed across the main hall.

Kaleus stood frozen. His eyes cloudy and lifeless. He turned again to look at Oberon and waited for him to speak.

#

Ilea felt the change in the people inside the castle. The music had stopped, and the soldiers were everywhere. She stopped fighting the butcher boxes and took a moment to rest. She flew down to one of the thin windows to peer into the castle. Jack and Nick and Zaldi stood in the center of the room. Soldiers pointed and moved in between the people, sending them out of the room and out of the castle. She could feel the lifesongs of her friends move out into the hallway, but they did not leave the castle. Instead, they hid with Syman and other men ... men she did not know. *Why are they here? Why are they in the castle? Did they find Jaika?*

Beneath her, Ilea watched a man move toward the center of the room with two cloaked figures. He shook them by their shoulders and yelled words that she could not hear. Then he jerked the hoods down from their heads. She could feel the hum of the butcher box tied to the young girl's waist. The king stood on the platform at the end of the room, and Ilea felt his heart twist with fear. *The girl beneath the cloak is special to him ... so much pain and fear ... maybe she is ... Jaika? That is why Jack and Nick are in this room.*

Beyond them, against the far wall, on a bench, Ilea could see Oberon looking smug and excited and arrogant. He stood and walked toward the center of the room. She could feel the hum of the SolStone he wore beneath his clothes. The SolStone she had left with Syman.

Ilea stiffened her back, raised her head, and turned to look behind her. In the distance she could feel the lifesongs of more than a hundred Tal. Adolphus and Seela, Tori and Dodgen and Kayz flew with them. They were coming to save the people from the explosives ... or maybe something else. Whatever Adolphus had spoken about. Whatever the people should prepare for ... was happening. He said it would happen tonight.

Ilea returned to the half-wall at the top of the tower and found a comfortable spot. She could feel the anger growing in the men below her. Angry men who could set off the explosives if they choose. There were still more devices in the city and the ones left below the castle. So many weapons to stop before the Tal arrived. Whatever was coming, Ilea wanted her friends with her, so her next task was to heal the device tied to Jaika.

#

Keshar stood outside the main hall watching Merith and Kaleus argue, while Galimar and his soldiers led the guests out of the castle through the kitchen and the side entrances. A lone rider carried the butcher box to the edge of town, but he knew there would be other explosives to find. Kaleus would not stop with just one.

Galimar ordered most of the soldiers toward the city wall with the guests, but he kept a handful of armed men close to the castle. Keshar had ordered them to stay out but to be ready for Kaleus's men when they showed. They could attack from anywhere. Galimar and his men watched in all directions with nervous fingers twitching on their burn guns.

Staggering, reeling from too much drink, a man wearing a cape complained. "Why are we leaving?" Then he grabbed onto one of the soldiers to keep from falling.

"I don't want to go!" another guest dressed in silver and blue shouted. "Where is my glass?"

Undaunted, the soldiers continued to pull and prod and guide the guests to safety.

Above the chatter of complaining voices, Galimar shouted to his men, "Keep moving the people toward the wall ... away from the castle! And watch for Kaleus's men!"

Galimar's soldiers spread out around the castle waiting for disaster. The enemy could be dressed as a guest or even another soldier. The attack could come from anywhere. They paced and twitched and looked behind them constantly ... waiting ... watching ... feeling their training in every heartbeat.

Then the sky filled with wings. Beneath the red moon, blue-skinned Tal who never left their mountain home fell from the sky to perch across the towers and walkways of the castle. The soldiers raised their weapons, but the sound of Galimar's voice kept them from firing ... at least for the moment.

#

Ilea felt the Tal closing in on the castle. Before she could hear the fury of wings, she could feel the power of their lifesongs. Her people landed across the top of the castle, here and there, polka-dotting the watch towers and the stone walls and the narrow melted-sand windows.

Adolphus landed beside her. She felt the weight of his lifesong as his feet touched the stone of the tower. She felt her mother and Dodgen land below her on the open walkways, and Kayz circling above the castle, refusing to land. And Tori ... she could feel Tori's lifesong above the others, reaching out to find her. Ilea hated the joy she felt at their arrival. Coming here could mean their deaths. There were still more weapons to disarm beneath the castle and others in the city. Her friends ... her family could be destroyed if the weapons released.

"I need more time," she whispered to Adolphus without looking up. Her focus remained on the final weapons.

She felt him turn and look down at the Tal and the Palon people shouting and pointing from the ground ... and the soldiers with their weapons raised.

Ilea stood and wrapped her arms around him, searching for her father's lifesong. "What do I do?" she wailed. "There are too many explosives ... too many butcher boxes. They will destroy the castle." She looked up into his hardened face. "Help me save them," she begged.

"Let me help." Tori landed beside Adolphus. "I can feel the stones ... the fire crystals in the city."

Dodgen and Kayz landed beside her, crowding together on the ledge.

Ilea backed away from Adolphus, her wings dragging the ground behind her. "There is not enough time. There are too many explosives ... not enough time."

"Until the city is gone, there is time," Tori argued. "Let us help."

Ilea took a deep breath. If they left now ... if they flew home, the Tal would be safe. Her family would be safe. *How can I ask them to give their lives?*

"Please," Tori tried again. "Let us help."

Ilea nodded. She knew she should send them away. They would all die if the boxes exploded, but maybe Tori was right. Maybe there was a chance. "Once you find them, the butcher boxes, you have to heal the stone. You can seal its power inside."

Tori bit her bottom lip not sure she could ever heal a fire crystal.

"If you cannot heal the stones, the butcher boxes must be carried out of the city."

"Who's going to do that?" Kayz whined.

"We can do it." Dodgen raised his shoulders then shoved Kayz sideways. "We can do it together. Right?"

Kayz smirked.

"And you." Dodgen looked up at Adolphus. "You can help too!" He shouted the words at the gray-eyed Tal.

"Yes," Adolphus agreed. He wasn't supposed to interfere. As a Krill, that was the pledge he had taken so long ago, but he had broken it over and over again. There was no reason to stop now. "Tori can lead the search within the city. I will help you find the weapons beneath the castle."

Ilea described the rafters and support beams that hid the weapons. The crates of ale that would burn and the stone columns that could collapse. "They won't be easy to find."

Dodgen winked at his sister. "You can trust us."

Adolphus spread his wings and flew from the rooftop to circle above the others. He shouted orders to the waiting Tal ... descriptions of the butcher boxes hidden in the city and beneath the castle, and how they could find them and destroy them. One by one the Tal rose into the sky to begin the search. Tori smiled at Ilea, then her wings lifted her from the half-stone wall as well. Dodgen and Kayz followed, calling out to the others to fly. The soldiers on the ground stared up at the Tal who followed Tori out into the city. But when Adolphus landed beside the castle entrance, Galimar's soldiers could no longer be still.

Ilea heard the soft *phffft* of the first burn round hit the stone above the doorway below her. She dove from the half-wall, holding her wings motionless behind her as she fell, the ground rushing toward her until her wings burst open to stop her fall. She landed beside Adolphus feeling Dodgen and Kayz drop behind her. Two more burn rounds exploded against the door frame. Adolphus ducked and pushed Dodgen and Ilea inside the castle. Kayz skittered along the stone, jumping and hopping from the ground to the door to the ceiling. Another burn round melted and dripped from the top of the door. Even though she knew they wouldn't listen, Ilea reminded her friends to be careful. Then she pointed to the stairs that would lead them beneath the castle to the butcher boxes and possibly their deaths. Her heart ached as she felt their lifesongs grow faint when they descended to the floors below.

Syman

Ilea took a deep breath then blew out her air, long and slow. Her eyes narrowed and her wings shuddered behind her as she started down the endless hallway toward Jack and Nick and whoever else needed her. As she neared the main hall, Keshar moved to pull his sword, but Syman stepped in front to block his attack. Zaldi reached down to grip Keshar's shoulder in case he misunderstood the warning.

Ilea paused beside Nick and Jack. Her eyes softened for a moment with the memories of their journeys together. She did not have the words to explain the butcher box or how it was healed, so she used the words she knew. "Your friend is safe. Jaika ... is safe." Then she continued into the main hall toward Kaleus and Oberon. The remaining Tal followed, creeping into the room. Hand and foot and claw, they climbed the walls and hung from the ceiling, waiting ... waiting. Keshar's mouth dropped open as they passed.

Merith jumped from his platform and drew his sword. "This is your doing!" he shouted to Kaleus. "You brought these filthy creatures into my home."

Keshar drew his sword as well and stepped out into the main hall, ready to fight the Tal.

Davin turned to glare at Oberon as he approached from the back wall. "What are you doing?"

Davin yelled. "Why are you here?" He motioned toward the ceiling. "You brought them, didn't you?"

"I came to save you." Oberon forced his back to straighten. "To tell you ... you are my son."

"Did you think I didn't know?" Davin's eyes narrowed. "Did you think I couldn't remember your visits to my mother ... how you left us with nothing. You kept us a secret because you were ashamed ... ashamed of me."

"No ... no, you don't understand. I was never ashamed of you."

"Oberon?" Merith couldn't believe his eyes. "You should be dead."

"No!" Oberon shouted. "It is you who will die!"

Davin stared at Oberon. He didn't trust him or Merith. He wanted them all dead.

"Finish this!" Oberon growled to Kaleus. "I will have my revenge."

But Kaleus just stared. His eyes lifeless and cold. Oberon pulled the SolStone from beneath his tunic. The blue light pulsed in his hand. *Not now,* he thought to the stone. *Don't control him. Let Kaleus go. Let him kill Merith.*

"End Merith's daughter!" Oberon growled.

Kaleus turned the detonator over and over in his hand. His mind at war with the SolStone's control. Jaika stiffened her body and readied for the explosion. Richard held his breath as Kaleus's fingers closed on the trigger … but nothing happened. The butcher box did not explode. Ilea smirked, and the rope that held Jaika's box dissolved. The weapon clattered as it dropped to the stone floor.

"Jaika!" Nick called out from behind Ilea, stepping closer and closer.

Jaika didn't think. She didn't think about the butcher box on the floor or her father or Richard. She stepped away from Kaleus and ran. Her cloak rippled as she ran past Ilea. With all the strength she had left, she threw her arms around Nick, buried her face against his neck, and waited for the world to end.

"How did you get here?" she whispered against his skin, her body shaking in his arms.

Richard stared at Jaika in this stranger's embrace, and the two men locked eyes across the main hall. The heartbreak in Richard's face was fleeting but unmistakable. Richard's eyes narrowed and his mouth tightened. Nick watched as this man's pain became hatred.

Nick pushed Jaika away, just enough to see her face.

271

Tears formed in the corners of her eyes. "I thought I'd never see you again."

"Ilea brought us here," Nick explained as he held her by the shoulders. "She saved you and me and Jack."

Zaldi stomped in the doorway behind them and a green-skinned woman dug her fingers into Jack's arm. Jaika reached up to run her fingers along the edge of Nick's scruff of a beard. Mattie and school and her life on Earth felt a million years away. Another life … another world … simply a dream. Then she stood on her tiptoes and kissed him. In the main hall, in front of Richard and Syman and Kaleus. She kissed Nick long and hard and full on the mouth, knowing they could die at any moment. Her secret no longer mattered.

"No!" Richard growled, then grabbed Kaleus by the throat. The two men fell to the ground, thrashing and shouting. Richard's fingers dug into the king's flesh, and he did not let go.

Oberon's eyes grew wide at the chaos. He lifted the SolStone above his head. "This is not the end. I will have revenge!" The blue light smoked above him, swirling and rising.

The ground beneath the castle began to shake.

Syman

Suddenly, Adolphus appeared beside Ilea. "There is not enough time."

Ilea could feel the hum of the fire crystals still below the castle. They had failed. Dodgen and Kayz were still searching for the butcher boxes. Her stomach felt hollow and empty. She closed her eyes and tried to find courage. "I cannot do this alone. I need your help." She knew what she was asking was unforgivable. She was asking for her father's death.

Adolphus nodded. The gray of his eyes faded to blue, and Ilea could feel her father, pure and whole and dying.

"Forgive me," she whispered, looking up into his fearless eyes. This would be the last time she would ever see her father. The last time she would hear him speak.

"I love you," he soothed. "Take the stone." Her father's voice was weak without the Krill. "Save the people."

Adolphus closed his eyes and breathed one last time. Ilea threw her arms around him as his body withered and crumpled to the stone floor.

"Forgive me," she begged as the silver light that was the Krill rose above his body then spiraled and split in two, releasing the white mist.

Her claws reached out to grasp the mist that was her father. The white mist that swirled upward, spiraling between her fingers, eluding her grasp. Her father rose and faded. The body beside her on the stone floor was now only a shell that held no life ... no warmth. The light that had been her father was gone.

"No!" she wailed as the tears scorched her cheeks.

Above her, the Krill burst into pinpoints of silvery light that spun and rose and dropped. Half of the light flew to the hallway to join with Syman. But the other half covered Ilea's face and hands and skin to become part of her. Just like her father, her eyes shifted from blue to gray. The pain of loss and defeat was now controlled by the Krill. She could hear its voice and her father's voice and a million other voices who had once known the Krill. Knowledge of past generations was hers for the taking.

She caressed her father's cheek. "I understand now."

Then she stood, without tears, and moved toward the center of the main hall. As she neared the others, Ilea pushed out her palm toward Oberon, and the SolStone in his hand began to shake.

Syman

Oberon gripped the stone with both hands. "Get away!" he shouted, as the blue light burst from between his fingers.

The stone shook and glowed with heat as it ripped from his hands. The stone flew to Ilea and sent Oberon reeling against the floor.

When Oberon fell, Jaika felt the heat of the light from her necklace burning against her skin. The pendant Inita had worn. The necklace Jaika had carried with her since her first day on Earth. She stepped away from Nick, broke the chain, and pulled it from beneath her tunic only to have it ripped from her fingers. She watched it join with the SolStone in the air above Ilea.

As the blue stone became whole, its light pulsed and grew. Ilea dropped to the floor, dug her claws into the stone, and released all that was her lifesong.

Nick pulled Jaika close again. "I've got you," he said. "Don't worry. I've got you." He didn't care what happened as long as they were together.

The blue light widened to fill the entire room. It moved and opened and extended beyond the castle and out into the courtyard were Galimar and his soldiers stood … out into the city where the merchants worked and the children slept … out to the edges of Palon. More than any doorway, the light covered and protected and began to transport the people.

Syman

The floor beneath them shook and dropped and crumbled in sections to leave open spaces to the room below. Syman's starburst of light erupted from the hallway. Joined by the silver light of the Krill, he became the dragon floating above Ilea. A massive black, winged animal, thicker, stronger, twice the size of before. His wings blocked the stones that sifted and fell from the castle ceiling. He hovered over her as the light grew. The Tal joined him. Rising from the walls, dropping from the ceiling, then hovered over him. Ilea drew a sharp breath and the light extended below the castle to reach Dodgen and Kayz, and then skyward, over the castle, upward to cover Syman and the Tal until everything was bathed in the light.

Syman roared as the heavy stones of the ceiling pounded against his bones, the Tal scattered, and the castle collapsed. The ground rumbled beneath the floor as the final butcher boxes exploded.

Ilea heard the roar of the explosion and felt the heat of its fire … then there was only the sand and the wind. The light had carried them away from the danger, out into the desert, and now it withdrew into the SolStone. There was only the people and the sand with Palon burning in the distance. The people turned to look in the direction of the city. The ground shook as explosions split the sky carrying with them rock and dirt and wood. All that was Palon exploded into the air.

Syman

The castle, the towers, the stone flew skyward then crumbled to the ground into nothing. Palon was gone.

Luna grabbed onto Jack's arm.

Nick held Jaika so tightly he thought his heart might burst.

Covered in sweat, his face bloody and scratched, Richard stared at Oberon cradling his scorched hands. The faded Guardian mumbled as he glared across the sand at the fallen city of Palon. Those who understood the sacred language of the Guardians would have heard him cursing Ilea and her ability to control the stone. They would have heard his pledge to destroy her ... to reclaim what was his.

Kaleus's lifeless body lay beside them in the sand.

King Merith fell to his knees, trying to understand what had happened. "She saved us." His eyes were wide and cold. "That blue skinned girl ... that filthy animal saved us." He laughed, giddy with fear and guilt. Merith's hands trembled with the knowledge that one Tal was capable of so much power. The Tal, who hid in the mountains. The Tal, who had raged war against his people so long ago.

Ilea stood, unharmed, beside the smoking ruins of the castle. The ground around her was scattered with fiery stones, charred cloth, broken glass and metal and wood and all that had been Palon. The smoke swirled and floated skyward. Ilea covered her nose to block out the bitter smell. She could feel the lifesongs of the Tal as they landed out in the sand with the rest of Palon: her mother, Dodgen, and Kayz among them. The soldiers, the merchants, the guests, even the prisoners who had been held beneath the castle stood on the sand ... but not Syman.

Ilea could feel his lifesong crushed beneath the weight of the castle stone. The Krill had been able to use Ilea and the SolStone to save the others, but not itself. She opened her wings and lifted from the ground, hovering over the debris, bathed in smoke and heat, feeling Syman struggle. Through the haze she could see the people of Palon in the distance, unaware of the Krill and its bravery. Without the dragon, she too would have been crushed beneath the stone.

Then, as she knew he would, Syman came apart. He burst into millions of tiny scatterbugs. Creatures with over a dozen legs and a body the size of a grain of sand. An endless stream of tiny feet ran in and out of the stones, in between the rocks and sand and wood and metal until they reached the larger spaces, where the scatterbugs joined together to become mice. Out of the rubble, out of the smoky haze, a thousand mice scampered from beneath the debris. Short legs carrying them in and out of the ruins. Long-tailed creatures that piled upon each other to become sparrows who then headed for the open sky. The sparrows rushed from the debris to meet in the red-mooned sky. A whirlwind of birds who then became the dragon.

Ilea understood all of these creatures through the eyes of the Krill.

Together, Ilea and the dragon flew to join the others out on the sand. Their wings, slow and heavy, carried them away from the fallen castle. Ilea could hear the Krill within her explaining that it could not stay divided and that remaining in Syman would result only in his death. So, as they landed on the sand, Ilea felt the silver light leave her and Syman to join and find another host.

She dropped to the sand and then to her knees. The emptiness left by the Krill washed over her body leaving behind a chaos of memories and voices that did not belong to her. Syman, who was no longer the dragon, reached down to help her stand. And then he smiled. Not because it was his duty or the correct protocol, but because he was happy. From his head to his toes, he smiled.

"So much I didn't know," he said. "So much I could not understand."

Ilea nodded, still trying to quiet the voices in her head. Amid the noise, Dodgen and Kayz and Tori landed beside her. Their lifesongs warm and wonderful. They chattered and laughed and asked her question after question.

"What happened?"

"Why did the castle explode?"

"And why are we here?"

"Because my daughter brought us here."

Ilea heard the voice of her mother and she could no longer be strong. "He's gone," Ilea cried as Seela wrapped her arms around her daughter's shoulders to pull her close. "Father is gone because of me."

Seela smiled softly, not believing for a moment that Ilea would hurt Adolphus. "But you are here. And we are here because of your courage. Your father would be so proud of you."

Ilea knew she spoke the truth. Her father's voice still echoed in her head. But her mother could not hide her own pain and emptiness at the loss of her husband, so Ilea felt the sadness two-fold ... her own as well as her mother's.

Then from out of the crowd of people, Ilea felt the presence of the Krill return. She wiped the tears from her eyes and pulled away from Seela. "Mother. These are my friends from Earth. These are the men who helped me to survive in the other world."

Jack stuck out his hand to shake and rambled on about mines and food and caves and magic. Seela found the patterns immediately and could understand every word. Jack shook Dodgen's hand and Kayz while Luna glimmered behind him, peering out at the Tal.

"We've been looking for Jaika for so long. We found a pink dog." Jack loosened his grip and, with a wide grin, he pointed to his friends. "This is Luna and Zaldi ... and Nick and that's Syman."

Ilea could hear Jack's voice as he chattered, but she could not take her eyes off of Nick. He removed his glasses and looked back at her with his cloudy, gray eyes. The same gray eyes that Adolphus had worn. The Krill now lived in Nick.

Jaika appeared beside Nick, caressing his back with her fingertips. "He was telling me about you." Jaika explained, trying not to cry. "About the bracelet and the lab and how you brought them here."

Ilea remembered their meeting in the great forest so long ago. The tiny girl hidden among the viney patch who offered her a blue stone bracelet.

"You were wrong about me," Jaika nodded. "You are the one who saved us." Then Jaika looked up at Nick and gripped his upper arm. "But something has happened to my Nick ... after the explosion. He is ..."

"Changed." Ilea finished her words. "I can explain, but it will take time."

"Time we do not have." Syman interrupted, staring at Jaika and the gray-eyed Nick standing beside her. "Regar cannot last much longer."

Above them, lights appeared in the sky. White and blue and red lights that seemed to go on forever. Behind them, Ilea could feel the soft hum of metal and machines ... and lifesongs.

"They are here." Nick nodded without emotion.

Ilea could feel Nick's lifesong mixed with the Krill. Nick was strong, stronger than her father had been, but he would never truly be the same once the Krill left him. She could feel Jaika's sadness, and Jack and Luna's joy, and the fear and dread of the others waiting out on the sand beneath the strange lights. Below her, she could feel the ground settling ... quieting ... controlled by the power that now lived in Nick. Nothing would ever be the same.

Syman

"Who is here?" Ilea asked, looking up at the sky. She could feel crystals and countless lifesongs behind those colored lights.

Nick pointed to the sky above them. "The Makers."

Syman

I would love to hear from you:
email me at
AlexRaeBooks@gmail.com

Watch for upcoming stories on
Facebook and Instagram
@AlexRaeBooks

Visit my website

https://alexraebooks.com/
to explore other books in the
Children of Regar series
and to receive a
FREE BONUS CHAPTER